TAVION SCOTT

MAJORING IN ME

ACCEPTANCE

Author: Tavion Scott
Cover Design: Red Raven Book Design
Publisher: Tavion Scott

© 2016 Tavion Scott. All rights reserved. This book or parts thereof may not be reproduced in any form, stored in any retrieval system, or transmitted in any form by any means—electronic, mechanical, photocopy, recording, or otherwise—without prior written permission of the copyright holder.

Printed in the United States of America

ISBN: 978-0-9974292-0-6 (Paperback edition)

ISBN: 978-0-9974292-1-3 (eBook edition)

This is a work of fiction. Names, characters, businesses, places, events and incidents are either the products of the author's imagination or used in a fictitious manner. Any resemblance or mention of real people, events, establishments, organizations, or locales are intended only to give the fiction a sense of reality and authenticity, or stems from pure coincidence.

TABLE OF CONTENTS

Acknowledgements..3

FRESHMAN YEAR

Chapter 1: Fall 2006..5

Chapter 2: Spring 2007..21

SOPHOMORE YEAR

Chapter 3: Fall 2007..50

Chapter 4: Spring 2008..97

JUNIOR YEAR

Chapter 5: Fall 2008..121

Chapter 6: Spring 2009...164

Going Forward...228

Ask For Help...229

Acknowledgements

    I first want to thank God for truly being my rock and guiding force throughout this writing journey. Despite not always being patient and the most appreciative of the bad times, which I now see as opportunities in disguise, you continued to love me and push me to reach for the dreams you placed within. Going forward, I pray that I'm more receptive and obedient to your word.

    I also want to acknowledge my mother. Although I've expressed my gratitude to her several times, I have to tell her again. Mom, thank you. Thank you for supporting me through this creative process. There aren't many moms out here that are as ride or die as you are, and I'm truly blessed to have you. Some people may be inclined to call me a mama's boy, but I don't care. Because lady, I love you and glad I was placed in your care those umpteen years ago.

    Last, but certainly not least, thanks to two friends and confidants that really encouraged me to keep writing. E.W., God knows you were a catalyst in me even picking up a pen and pad. You believed I could do this before I did. I'm still amazed that you were so confident in my writing. And C.R., you and I have been like two peas in a pod since we met. You've always had my back and always kept it real with me. You were never afraid to give me your honest feedback, and that was and is much appreciated. I'm grateful to have you both in my life.

Freshman year

Chapter 1: Fall 2006

August 26, 2006 (Saturday)

  I'm not sure what I expected my first college dorm to look like, but I know I definitely didn't expect this. When I went on a tour of Hamilton University, the dorm room my tour group viewed was decorated from wall to wall and smelled of vanilla. The room I stand in now is covered in off white cinder blocks, the kind found in prison cells; and, it smells like an indoor pool. There are two bare twin mattresses on opposite sides of the room, and matching computer desks and chairs. If I'm going to try to make this my home away from home for the next year, I have some work to do.

  "Tristan, what do you think?" my mom asks, standing next to one of the desks. I can tell she isn't quite impressed with my new living situation, but is trying to be as supportive as possible. I'm her only child, and as much as it pains her to see me leave the "nest," she understands I need to go to college and get the full college experience. Besides, I'm going to school in Alexandria, which will literally be forty-five minutes away from her.

  "It's cool," I reply. I'm not that impressed with the room either, but I'm trying to present a strong front for the lady of my life. "I'm going back downstairs to get some more of my stuff out the car."

  "Okay I'll help you, but let me tell you something first," my mom says. "I'm extremely proud of you for making it here Tristan. Can't believe I'm moving you out of my home and into a new one. Who knew those eighteen years would go by so fast?"

"Mom this is my dorm. Home is still home."

"Well, don't forget that," she smirks. "Hate for you to become a stranger."

"I won't," I say. I give her a big hug because I know she could use one.

"Alright Tristan, now they didn't give us much time to park the car in that spot, and I know you want to be done before Carter arrives, ready to move in." Carter is a guy I graduated high school with earlier this year. We don't really know each other that well, but we had mutual friends in high school; so, we decided to request to live together because we thought we would rather live with someone we knew a little, than with someone we didn't know at all. What I do know of him, he seems like a pretty decent guy. And despite being from a very wealthy family, he's not a stuck up snob.

On the way down to my mom's car to get some of my things, a girl walks through the entrance of the dorm floor with a box in her arms.

"Hi there, I'm Katie," the girl greets as she approaches us. "I live in room 212 down the hall. Looks like we are going to be floor mates." My mom's bottom jaw drops in shock. I hope she can pull it together here, and not embarrass me.

"Yeah I guess we are. I'm in room 218," I respond. "By the way, I'm Tristan."

"Nice to meet you," she smiles.

"And I'm his mother, Ms. Steele," my mom interjects.

"Of course, ma'am," Katie mumbles. "Nice to meet you too. Tristan I've got to go put this box down, it's getting kind of heavy. So I guess I'll see you around. Good bye Ms. Steele."

"See ya," I reply. She then bops down the hall to her room. Meanwhile, my mom is practically staring a hole in the side of my head.

"Mom I'm just as stunned as you are. I had no idea that this dorm is co-ed. Carter and I picked this dorm because his older brother told him this would be the best place to live as a freshman."

"Mmhmm," she grunts. "Just make sure you stay on the straight and narrow and don't make me a premature grandma." I can't do anything but shake my head and grin. We again start making our way back downstairs.

****

It's now sometime after 6:30pm and my mom has gone home. All but one person on my dorm floor has moved into their room. Those of us present in the dorm received a notification under our door earlier about a floor meeting in the lobby. As we gather in the lobby, I sit next to Carter naturally because I know him. He is a sun-kissed white guy slightly shorter than me and would be described by most as slightly thicker than average. Not to be confused with fat. Quite a few people in high school thought he looked like Shia LaBeouf the actor for some reason. Even squinting, I could never see the resemblance.

On the other side of me sits a new face. I figure she sat next to me because I, like her, am black. Whenever black people are placed in predominantly white environments, they

Majoring in Me   8

tend to gravitate toward like-faced individuals. It's all about trying to find something familiar in new surroundings where you may be labeled the "other." Anyway, this girl is tall, thin, chocolate brown, and stunningly beautiful. I wouldn't be surprised if she did, or wants to do some modeling.

Once everyone finds a seat, a short, straggly hair white man steps in front of our newly collegiate group. He looks like he literally rolled out of bed, threw on a wrinkled black shirt and some slightly stained light gray pants, and walked out here to the meeting. I wouldn't usually care about someone else's appearance, especially in a setting like this; but, I keep thinking about what my mom said about first impressions. I'm not sure he is making the best one as our residential advisor. I know he's that much by the big white lettering on his shirt that reads "Hamilton R.A., How can I help you?"

"Hey guys, my name is Steven and I'll be your R.A. for the year, or at least semester." He comes off very lethargic and quite monotone. "I'm the guy you come to when…" Just that quickly I start to tune him out, and take stock of all the people that would be living with me. As far as diversity went, it seems this mystery girl beside me, some guy across the circle, and I are the only blacks on this floor. There were two Latinos, and a couple of people of Asian heritage, but the room is mostly white. Upon completion of my examination of the room, I tune back into Steven in time to hear him propose that we do some kind of ice breaker activity.

"Ok, so we can get to know each other, let's go around the room and introduce ourselves. Just state your name, where you're from, your major if you have one, and a hobby." Typically, I hate these types of things. I always feel like I have to search for the perfect answers and give the perfect delivery. Why can't we just get to know one another the old fashion way?

****

Before I know it, we've gone around most of the room, and it's now Carter's turn to speak. "I'm Carter West, I'm from Manassas, Virginia, I'm a business major, and I'm single ready to mingle ladies." I know Carter is attempting to be funny, but he is coming across as a bit pompous and a little slimy. To me at least. However, several people appear to find humor in his introduction, especially a few girls. It's now my turn to introduce myself.

"I'm Tristan Steele, also from Manassas, and I'm majoring in Criminology. And as far as a hobby, I love to watch the NBA. I'm definitely a Cleveland Cavalier fan," I say. I feel like I gave a real generic and bland response, but heck, I didn't really know what to say, and didn't want to do this. I'm glad to be done.

"Hi, I'm Denise Jones," the black girl next to me states with a southern twang I only hear when visiting my relatives in the heart of Alabama. "I'm from a small town in Virginia called Danville, and I haven't decided on a major yet. I like watching basketball too," she says, looking in my direction. "I actually use to play back in high school." And with Denise finishing up the group "ice breaker," I'm left thinking I would make very few friends on my floor, and perhaps in college altogether. It didn't sound like I have many things in common with most of my new living companions. At least Denise and I have basketball to build a foundation of friendship on, and Carter is someone I kind of know already. I guess only time will tell what my college social life will look like going forward.

November 3, 2006 (Friday)

    I'm a little over half way into my first semester at Hamilton, and I'm just starting to fit in around here. I've stopped going home every weekend and settled into this living arrangement with Carter. Well, almost. As an only child use to his own bedroom and own habits, it took some adjusting to all of a sudden share a space with another person. Especially Carter.

    Carter has turned out to be quite the college stereotype. He spends more time at parties than in class, his side of the room looks like a disaster zone, and the number of girls he has managed to sleep with in the few months that we've been here would shock even the world's biggest playboy. He and I may be total opposites, but his lifestyle and slobbish ways aren't what have been the hardest for me to adjust to. As long as his clothes and things stay on his side of the room and they don't smell, that's none of my business. It's someone eating all my Toaster Pops that I still can't wrap my mind around.

    You would think, as well off as his family is, Carter would regularly go to the store in between his busy socialite schedule, and purchase his own snacks. Some days I came to the room from class hoping to put one of the packs of fruit jelly filled pastries in the microwave, and to my surprise I had none. Since I'm trying to avoid any and all conflict in my living situation, I haven't confronted him directly about it. Instead, I've started hiding a box of toaster pastries in my underwear drawer. He won't dare go in there.

    If I'm honest with myself, minus the snack situation, Carter has actually been a solid roommate. When we do happen to be in the room at the same time, we surprisingly have pretty good conversations. We talk about old times in high school, what happened at the latest party he attended, and his flavor of the week. Plus, he has never asked me to leave the room anytime he's wanted to entertain. He usually goes to the girl's place.

Outside of Carter, I've actually tried getting to know the rest of my floor, but to almost no avail. Based on the things I've seen, my floor is reminiscent of a season of MTV's *The Real World*. Several people on my floor have a sex partner on this floor. And most of the people I'm living with have awakened on several Saturday afternoons with a massive hangover. Being the odd ball out, thankfully I found a kindred spirit in Denise.

Over the past few months, she and I have become quite good friends, in the most platonic of ways. I think our friendship was accelerated because we both didn't have a real desire to have casual sex or party or drink, so we often would hang together. Denise has no interest in letting the boys in our hall, or at Hamilton for that matter, into her "cookie jar." She actually has a boyfriend that attends James Madison University. My new college friend also didn't find it wise to get hammered on a continual basis so early into her collegiate career.

As for why *I've* stayed away from all the partying and hookups, one has to know me. And not that many people here know me yet. I grew up as the "good boy" or "goody two-shoes." I have never drank, never smoked, and never have had an interest in "banging" as many girls as possible. Heck, I am still a virgin. I've never gone on a real date, nor had a real girlfriend. However, I always reason that I'm staying focused on school, and girls are a distraction. Carter asks me every now and then how I can manage not getting any. Oddly enough, I've never felt an aching in my pants for any girl, so I manage just fine.

Anyways, tonight Denise and I are about to walk to Liberty Arena to watch Hamilton's men's basketball team play its first home game. We came up with the brilliant idea to go to the game, and then afterwards walk to the McDuff's Burgers across the street and pig out on the Cheap Eats Menu. We often tried to eat off campus on the weekend to get away from the weekday usual.

"Hey Denise, are you ready?" I ask while standing in the hallway outside of her room.

"Yeah sure," she answers. "Just let me put on my shoes." I've gotten accustomed to waiting on Denise whenever we plan to go out. I don't mind the waiting as long as we aren't late. "Alright Tristan, let's go!" We begin the twenty minute trek from our dorm to Liberty Arena. Usually when we go on such walks, we talk about what's going on with our classes and what's happening within the relatively small black community here on campus.

"Did you start writing that paper for Professor Madison's class yet?" Denise questions. "It's due in like a month." If only my friend knew that ever since high school, I've never been the type to start a paper early.

"Oh, did you start working on it?" I deflect. "What's your topic?"

"I see you and I are in the same boat," she responds. "We're both procrastinating." We both just laugh. "So let me ask you another question. Do you still like that Kari chick?"

"Naw, I think I'm over her," I chuckle. Kari Green has to be the prettiest girl in the freshman class. She has flawless brown skin, a great body, and definitely knows how to dress. Unfortunately, Kari knows all of this. Often times she comes off pretentious and self-centered. As a result, Denise is not Kari's biggest fan. She thinks Kari is shallow and slightly stuck up. However, I made a point to tell Denise and Carter that I liked her. While I did find her gorgeous, I didn't really like her romantically. I just told Denise and Carter that so I would stop getting probed about my love life.

"Good," Denise says. "You can do much better."

"Is that right?" I counter.

"Yep," she replies. "It sure is. Now on to this pledging thing. Did you think any more about trying to pledge Alpha Epsilon Theta?" My friend definitely knows how to switch up the topics of conversations.

"I mean, I think I want to be an Alpha Ep. I just have to get to know some of the guys on campus," I respond. Before arriving to Hamilton University, I set in my mind that I would join Alpha Epsilon Theta Fraternity. I told myself that I want to join this brotherhood because it had been such an instrumental part of the civil rights movement in the 1950s and 1960s. Also, my high school counselor was an Alpha Ep man, and he's been a great mentor in my life. These two things, compounded by the fact I heard from family and friends that I look like I should be in this fraternity, made me interested in pursuing it.

"What about you?" I continued. Did you think any more about pledging a sorority?"

"Now you know how I feel Tristan. I thought about joining a sorority one time, but then I remembered I have a sister and really don't need anymore. Plus, what do I look like paying for sisterhood when I have one for free." We both chuckle and continue walking.

****

"Tristan, why would you let me eat that much at McDuff's?" Denise asks.

"Well you are the one that said you wanted to celebrate the team win," I answer. "Besides, we will go to the gym tomorrow and work it off." That's my half-ass attempt to reassure Denise she would not gain the infamous Freshman Fifteen.

"Next time, be a friend and tell me I may want to ease up on that menu," she giggles before unlocking the door to our dorm. "I'm going to go wrap my hair and call Jason so I can go to bed." Jason is Denise's boyfriend. I don't think Jason likes me that much, albeit we have never met. Denise told me that he always acts funny when she mentions my name. I understand why he's not fond of me though. He probably thinks I'm trying to get with Denise; but, that is the furthest thing from my mind. This girl has become like my sister.

"Alright then," I say. "Don't tell Jason you went to the game with me. I don't want to be the cause of no mess." While I'm smirking, she's giving me a side eye like only she could give. She then walks down the hallway toward her room.

"Night, boy!"

December 16, 2006 (Saturday)

With my first semester behind me, I'm back at home in Manassas for the winter break. Even though Denise and I have only been apart for a week, it feels weird not seeing my partner in crime every day. However, we are both spending time with our families and hanging out with our old friends.

"Mom, is the clock on the stove right?" I ask.

"Yeah, it should be," she replies.

"Okay thanks. I've got to get ready to go then. I told Alex I would meet him, Isaac, and Darius at eight."

"Oh alright hun. So where are you guys going tonight?

"Isaac suggested we go play pool at Hard Times Café, so I think we are going there. And I already know before you say it: I'll be careful." My mom isn't strict or anything, she just wants me to be cautious.

"Well as long as you know," she says. "Do you need some money for gas or something?" I appreciate this woman. She knows I am an unemployed college student, and could use some funds. My mom suggested I don't work my first year in college. She thinks I should see how I'm able to deal with a full time student course load before adding more to my plate. I on the other hand really want to work because we, as in my mom and I, are not exactly rolling in the dough. I hate having to take money from my mom, but I took her advice and remain a student only. For now anyway.

"Um maybe," I respond.

****

"Alright Mom, I'm out," I yell as I run down the stairs toward the front door. "Thanks again for the money.

"No problem, just be careful," she reiterates, as I walk out the door.

Getting in my car to head over to meet the guys, the first thing I do is pop in my favorite album into the CD player. The album is no other than *B'Day*. My love for Beyoncé and her music is something that I've kept as a closely guarded secret. If folks discover my secret love, they will make the assumption that I'm gay. Especially the very guys I'm on my way to see. I foolishly bought into the notion that there are certain artists that are off limits for straight guys to like, unless they want their sexuality called into question. Beyoncé happens to be one of those artists, along with Britney Spears and Jennifer Lopez. Wanting to get my private Beyoncé fix however, I blast her all the way down the parkway until I pull into the Hard Times Café parking lot.

Entering through the doors of Hard Times Café, I notice I'm the first one to get here. I'm usually the first one to arrive to things, so I'm not sure why I expected this time to be any different.

"Hi sir, did you want a table?" the blonde hostess asks.

"No thank you," I respond. "I'm actually waiting on the rest of my friends to get here. I think we are just going to go in the back and play pool."

"Okay," she says. "Let me know if you need anything." She then goes back to straightening the menus at the hostess stand.

After waiting ten minutes, I decide to pull out my phone to send a text to the guys letting them know I made it here. Looking toward the back of the place, I can see that the pool tables are starting to get crowded. All I can do is hope my friends get here soon, so we can actually get a table.

"Ay T-man," a voice calls out. Turning my head, I see that the voice belongs to Alex. "T-man" had become my nickname in our crew. Alex is about my height and my complexion. We usually refer to him as Lex. Out of the crew, he's the most thorough about knowing random facts, especially about sports. He decided to take a year off from school before going to college so he could figure out what he wanted to do. So for now, he is working at the mall.

"What's up, Lex?" I greet as I dap him up. "What took you guys so long to get here?"

"Man, my parents decided they wanted me to do some things around the house right before I was getting ready to go," Alex answers. "And it's not like I can tell them no," he laughs. "Like my folks always say, they pay the mortgage."

"I hear you," I reply.

"But yo man, you're still swole," Alex continues. Out of my friends, I have the more muscular physique. Back in the day, I used to wrestle and run track, and since those days I've made an effort to stay in relatively good shape.

"Lex chill," I counter. "I'm just not trying to gain weight, but this dude Duck got huge." I'm referring to Darius. I can't actually remember why we call him Duck, but we've been calling him that for what seems like forever. Darius is both lighter in complexion and taller than Alex and I. He used to be quite skinny, but today he is visibly more built. His chest is almost bigger than mine.

Now, Darius is the jerk of our clique. He is the one that typically says what we are all thinking, but know we shouldn't say because someone's feelings may get hurt. Unfortunately, he lacks that tact. Darius is currently enrolled at Norfolk State University. Based off the text messages I received this past semester, it's safe to assume that his experience at an HBCU is quite different from mine at a PWI. But that's to be expected.

"T-Man, you're just shrinking," Darius jokes. "Y'all ready to go get a table so we can play pool or what?"

"Whoa wait a minute," Alex orders. "We got to wait on this guy Isaac. He sent me a text right before I left, said he was on the way."

"That nigga is forever running late," Darius points out. "Twenty bucks that he texts one of us in like five minutes saying he's not coming." If Isaac does text one of us with this message, it wouldn't be the first time. Out of the crew, he is the only one with a girlfriend. That being said, sometimes he had to bail on hanging with us to spend time with his lady. But before anyone could take Darius up on his bet, Isaac walks through the door.

"Isaac," Alex welcomes. "What's going on playa?"

"Not much Lex," Isaac answers. "My bad for being late. I had to drop my little sister off at the movies." Isaac is the tallest of us all, standing at around 6'4". He is of mixed heritage—his mom is Puerto Rican and his dad is black. Isaac is most assuredly the lightest in complexion and has a lanky basketball player build. If Darius is the most candid, then Isaac has to be the most argumentative out of my group of friends. For some reason, he likes to argue. Even when he is wrong, he thinks he is right. Isaac is also currently enrolled at an HBCU. He attends Savannah State University, in Georgia.

"Finally, the crew is back together," Alex exclaims.

****

Having finally started playing pool, Darius decides to make a little small talk.

"Ay T-man, you smashing them females up at Hamilton?" he brashly asks. The guys know that I'm the lone virgin of the group, and I guess they thought this would change now that I'm in college.

"Naw Duck," I mumble. "You know I'm still trying to save myself till marriage." I can't help but wish that someone would quickly change the topic of conversation. As an eighteen year old male virgin, in a crew where all of my friends have prior sexual experience, I feel like I have three eyes and a horn on the top of my head. As crazy as it may sound, I feel slightly embarrassed.

"T-man," Isaac chimes in. "You're not getting in all those snow bunnies at Hamilton?" By now I am desperately wanting to talk about the weather, sports, or anything really. My lack of sexual experience, and furthermore my lack of pursuit of such, while noble to some, is awkward in this group.

"Hey Duck, what happened to that girl you said you were talking to a few weeks ago?" Alex jumps in. Man do I appreciate him right about now.

"Lex which girl you talking about?" Darius replies. Darius probably does need to be reminded of which girl Alex is referring to, because Darius is no stranger to the opposite sex. Since he's been at Norfolk, he's allegedly become quite the ladies' man.

"Never mind fool," Alex sighs as the rest of us chuckle. "Just don't catch anything or get some girl pregnant."

****

Before I know it, we leave Hard Times Café and get in our respective cars. Once in my car, instead of blasting my secret love, I opt to ride in silence and do some thinking. I can't help but to contemplate all the reasons why I'm holding onto my virtue. Beyond focusing on school, there is the fact that I'm trying to save myself until marriage. I know it's old school and somewhat laughable these days for men, but I can't get my Sunday school teacher's words out of my head. "Save yourself for marriage, God and your bride will appreciate it."

Then there is the extreme awkwardness I feel around the opposite sex. It isn't awkward for me around Denise, because while a gorgeous girl, I've never viewed her as a potential mate. Can't say why that is exactly, and I've never really questioned it.

For some reason, when I get around most women I feel myself trying to mimic the kind of guy I know they desire. The girls I like are always drawn to the guy that is confident, humorous, slightly an asshole, and that behaves as if he is skilled enough to get any lady he wants. However, my mimicking attempts of this type of man often feels weird and fraudulent. Rightfully so, since in essence I'm trying to create inorganic chemistry. Regardless of the true reasoning as to why I am a still a virgin, the fact that I am a virgin is something that is not changing anytime soon.

Chapter 2: Spring 2007

January 22, 2007 (Monday)

    It is the day before my second semester of college, and I'm back at Hamilton with my sister Denise. To celebrate our reunion, we decided to come off campus to The Green Tortilla. I introduced Denise to the place last semester, and she's been hooked ever since.

    "Tristan, what are you getting?" she asks me as we stand in line at the Mexican American restaurant.

    "You know I'm getting my usual, a burrito bowl with chicken." I never really stray too far into the menu.

    "I've been craving that steak burrito bowl something serious," Denise giggles. "You know they don't have a Green Tortilla back home."

    Once we order our food, Denise and I sit down at one of the tables near the back of the restaurant. While I'm practically wolfing down my food, Denise stops eating hers. She starts looking at me as if she has something to get off her chest.

    "So Tristan, I have some news for you. I am officially single." I stop eating because I'm stunned by the news.

    "Single," I gasp.

"Yeah you heard me right. Single. Jason and I just weren't meant to be."

"Wow," I sigh. "Are you okay?"

"I'll be okay. Trust me," She assures me. "I'm actually better off without the asshole."

"Well look at you," I say. "I'm glad you're alright. You must have been listening to Beyoncé's 'Irreplaceable.'" I don't fear my sexuality would be questioned making this reference, because the song's been playing everywhere. I'm sure men and women, straight and gay, know it.

"You damn right," Denise exclaims. "Throwing him to the left. Pack his bags. All of that!"

"So if you don't mind me asking, what happened?" I further inquire. Call it curiosity, but I'm wondering what put the final nail in that relationship. Denise and Jason had been together since freshman year of high school. I know they've had their share of disagreements, and that at times Jason can be a real jerk, but I always thought they would stay together no matter what.

"Do you want the short version or long version?" she counters.

"Long please," I chuckle.

"You got it," she giggles. "So it all started New Year's Eve, when Jason and I decided to go out to this eighteen and up spot with my girl Aja and her boyfriend Nate. Jason volunteered to drive all four of us up there."

"Maybe I want the short version instead," I interrupt jokingly.

"How about I just speed it up rudeness," she quips. "In the club the four of us were dancing, and that's when some girl walked up to Jason. Tristan, she had to have the biggest butt I have ever seen on such a little body. If she wasn't so handsome in the face, I would have sworn she got work done."

"Timeout," I interject. "Handsome?"

"Yes Tristan, handsome. You know I'm not one to ever call anyone ugly, because they say your future kids will come out and look just like that person. So if I don't find a girl particularly pretty, and believe her to have the features of the world's first man, I say handsome." I again start laughing out loud.

"Where did you get this stuff from friend?" I ask.

"My grandma," she answers. "Who else? Well anyway, this girl started hugging up on him, and talking about how good it was to hang with him at some party at his school two months ago. I mean, she acted as if she didn't see me standing there."

"Wow that's bold," I gasp.

"That's what I thought," she animatedly says. "What kind of woman rolls up on a man that is obviously with his girlfriend? When the girl walked away from Jason, you know I started playing fifty questions. He swore up and down to me this girl was just a friend of his roommate. I didn't fully believe him, but I dropped it because I didn't want to ruin the rest of my night. I refused to go into the New Year on a bad note."

"The mystery girl is why you two broke up?" I ask.

"If you let me finish the story, you'll find out," she giggles.

"My bad, Denise."

"No problem boy. So three days after that night at the club, I was with Aja at the mall. We were passing by the food court, and I see Jason sitting at a table with this girl. Aja wanted to bust his head right there, but I calmed her down because I wanted to see how he was going to lie to me. Aja and I rolled up to the table, and he looked upset while the girl looked real comfortable."

"I asked Jason directly what was going on. The girl tried to dismiss herself, but Aja stepped behind her chair so she couldn't get up. And that's when all the information started pouring out. Tristan, he slept with this girl, and apparently got her pregnant."

I for one was not expecting that bomb shell. Cheating is complicated enough without adding a child into the mix. I have more than a few follow up questions, but I'm hesitant to ask.

"Tristan, when I heard a baby was on the way, I knew then it was over. Instead of cussing Jason out or attacking the mother of his child, I just told him to consider us done and walked away. I'm never going to be that girl that comes out of pocket in public. Unfortunately for him, Aja didn't share my sentiment. She slapped him in the back of the head before leaving, and wished the girl good luck with 'pencil dick.'" I think I just choked on my food.

"Denise she did not?"

"I promise you I'm not lying," she smiles. "I have a ride or die friend in Aja."

I guess you do," I reply. "Sorry he did that to you."

"I'm cool Tristan. Really. I've already cried and been through my 'I hate men' faze. Jason tried calling me a bunch of times to apologize and get back together. But I can't go back to that dysfunctional and outdated relationship. Especially, when he has a kid coming. So it's time to just move on."

"Good for you," I exclaim.

As we continue to eat our food and discuss the time we spent at our respective homes with our families and friends, I start thinking about my plans for this new semester. Outside of going to class and eating on campus with Denise and Carter, I was for the most part inactive in the Hamilton community this past fall. I want to change that.

"Hey Denise, I feel like I have to get more involved on campus."

"Oh yeah," she replies. "That sounds like a plan for me too. We gotta meet some more of the people at this school, especially the black ones."

"Right," I agree. "I want to be more than just a student." This is a very true statement. I was very involved in high school. I was captain of the track team, president of the Peer Mediators Club, and member of the National Honor Society. So being in college and not involved in extracurricular activities is a bit strange to me. Although I think I want to become a member of Alpha Epsilon Theta, it's not something that I could just join. My membership in that organization depends on a variety of factors, some of which are out of my control.

"Okay, so what were you thinking of joining?" Denise inquires.

"Well, I was looking at the Student Activities board outside of the Student Center earlier today, and I saw a flyer for Hamilton's Black Student Awareness Society meeting.

Apparently they have their first meeting of the semester on Thursday. Do you want to go?"

"Sure why not," she answers. "Maybe I can find me a new man."

"Maybe," I chuckle.

January 25, 2007 (Thursday)

It's 7:00pm, and Denise and I are on the way to the Black Student Awareness Society meeting. I'm not sure what to expect from this meeting. I hope that not only would I be compelled to join this group, but that I would meet some more of the black students at Hamilton too.

"Um Denise, it looks like we should have gotten here a little earlier," I say as we enter the very packed A. Philip Randolph Room. I can't recall seeing this many people that look like me all at once on campus. Gazing upon the numerous faces in the room, I notice several black fraternal Greeks I had seen around the university. For example, there's Bradley. He is the president of Alpha Epsilon Theta Fraternity, and quite popular on campus. Also, I peep three of the twenty-five members of Sigma Delta Zeta Sorority. Turning my head further, I notice the "big man" on campus, Ben Watkins. He's a member of Kappa Nu Omega Fraternity, an inspiring R&B singer, and to most females on campus, the most eligible bachelor at our school. As Denise spots him, she leans over to me.

"I should have gotten here earlier so I could get a seat next to him," she whispers. I just roll my eyes.

"Welcome to the first BSAS meeting of the new year," yells Cassandra Brown. Cassandra may be short and petite, but she is surprisingly loud. "I'd like to get this meeting started by talking about BSAS' plans for Black History Month, as it literally starts in less than a week.

****

After roughly an hour went by, the meeting is now coming to a close and those BSAS members that belong to other organizations start plugging different events sponsored by their respective groups. In the midst of such plugs, I see this short and stout guy stand up.

"Hello everyone, I'm Chance" he says with almost perfect diction. "I just wanted to announce that Blessed Voices of Triumph will be having choir rehearsal this Sunday at 6:00pm. As the assistant director, I can say that we would love to have new members." At that announcement, I lean over to Denise.

"I may have to check that choir thing out," I whisper. "You trying to roll with me?"

In Denise fashion, she gives me a perplexed look and replies, "I've been blessed with many things, but a voice isn't one of them. You will have to go to that one on your own brotha!"

"Alright got ya," I snicker. While I'm disappointed Denise isn't going to go with me, I understand. I really want to go to the rehearsal, because it's been a while since I was in a gospel choir, and I miss it.

Following Chance's announcement, everyone in the room heads to the door. Before Denise and I leave though, I want to at least introduce myself to Bradley the Alpha Ep since I am interested in joining his brotherhood. Now I know better than to tell him outright in a room full of people my interest in membership. The research I found online and my high school counselor cautioned me against that. But I at least want to make myself known. However before I introduce myself to him, I have to figure out what I'm going to say, so I don't come off weird. Again, first impressions. Then it hits me.

"Hey what's up man," I greet Bradley as I dap him up without embracing him like I would with my friends from back home. "Weren't you an orientation leader over the summer?"

"Yeah I was," he replies. "I think I remember seeing you at one of the orientation sessions. You're a freshman right?"

"Yep I'm a freshman," I respond, glad that he remembers my face. "I figured I would get involved on campus, so I came to the meeting tonight."

"Cool, cool. That's what's up bruh? What's your name again?"

"Oh I'm Tristan Steele."

"Nice to meet you," Bradley says as he extends his hand to me as if to dap me up again. "I actually have something to do with frat that I'm late for. But if you're free two Saturdays from now, my chapter is hosting a community service project at the church down the street. If you want to go, just message me on AirNote."

"Okay sounds good, thanks," I respond. "Have a good one!"

"You too Tristan."

As I walk back over to Denise, I'm slightly excited. I know that I accomplished a successful introduction. And via this introduction, I took my first steps in becoming a man of Alpha Ep.

"That looked like it went well," Denise says. I nod with a smug look on my face. "But Tristan, can you consider becoming a Kappa Nu instead, so you can hook a sista up with that fine ass Ben Watkins?" At that, I scoff at Denise's request and we both make our way to the exit.

January 28, 2007 (Sunday)

Sunday is finally here, and I'm headed to the Blessed Voices of Triumph choir rehearsal. I'm slightly nervous about going though. I fear that I may not be up to par with the vocal talent there. I mean, I can carry a tune, and outside of the shower at that, but I'm not sure if I'll fit in. Also, I wonder what the members will be like. If they will welcome me with open arms, or if they will give me a cold shoulder as the new guy.

Opening the door to the choir room, I see thirty-five shades of blackness with a few shades of white and brown. Within the crowd of people, I only count about six guys. Although I was hoping for more male representation, I'm appreciative of the six that are here. Walking toward an available seat in the assumed baritone/tenner section, I nod at the various choir members, signifying my hello.

"Alright folks, let's get started and open up in prayer," Chance says. After the prayer, he takes the time to make a few announcements and calls for new members to stand and introduce themselves. I'm one of four people to stand up per the request. Once the four of us "newbies" told the room our short bio, Chance welcomes us and soon begins to work with the soprano section on a new song. While directing these ladies to my left, two of the guys in front of me start conversing with one another before turning around to me.

"So Tristan, you're from Manassas right?" one of the guys asks.

"Sure am," I answer. "And you man? By the way, what's your name?

"Oh my bad," he replies. "I'm Kirk and this is Elan." Kirk points to the guy he was previously speaking with before turning to me. "We both are from Virginia Beach. Hey man, you ball? Saturdays around noon, me, Elan, and a few of our friends go to the Powerhouse and play pick-up games. You should come." While I appreciate the invite, Kirk has no idea that I can't really play basketball.

"Thanks man," I tell him. "I love watching college and professional ball, but trust me when I tell you, you don't want to see me play. I definitely defy that stereotype." All of us just quietly laugh at my joke. That small joke served as a segue into a conversation about Lebron James and the current NBA season.

When Chance finally exhausts the voices of the girls in the soprano section, he takes a quick break to regroup. Coincidentally, as he sits down to take a break, a fairly tall and light brown guy walks through the door. He has on a stylish black trench coat with skinny blue jeans and a white button up shirt. On the top of his head is a Mohawk. I can tell he has quite the personality as he walks past the girls of the choir, telling them a quick comedic anecdote that left each of them giggling. Finally approaching the guys' section, he sits down in the chair right next to me.

"Hello sir, how are you?" he greets me. "I'm Bryan, and you are?" His hand extends out to me.

"I'm Tristan, nice to meet you." I can't put my finger on it, but something about this handshake with Bryan is slightly peculiar.

*****

With rehearsal over for the night, I'm getting ready to walk across the campus back to my dorm. Before I can leave, several of the choir members come up to me to exchange parting words, including Kirk and Bryan. I'm relieved to have such a warm reception amongst the members. And more importantly, I'm glad I didn't feel out of my league being here vocally. My prior nerves about this evening were definitely unwarranted.

"Don't worry, I'll be back next week," I yell walking out of the door, after Chance asked if I would be attending future choir rehearsals. Heading back to my room, I can't help but think about how good this group sounded tonight. I mean it's no Mississippi Mass Choir, but it's definitely impressive. Even to the most musically trained ear.

****

Arriving in front of my room, the door flings open before I have a chance to insert my key. Carter is standing in the doorway.

"Hey roommate, what's happening?" Carter asks as he buttons his winter coat.

"Not much," I answer. "Just finished up rehearsal for that choir I told you about. Where you off to?"

"Oh boy Tristan! I finally got that girl on the second floor to go out with me. So I'm on my way to pick her up, and we're heading to the movies. Hopefully, I'll see you sometime tomorrow if you know what I mean." With this smug expression on Carter's face, how could I not know what he means? We chuckle, and he walks out the door.

Wanting to just relax while Carter's out of the room, I hop in my bed and jump on my laptop. Like many college students, I find myself relaxing by web surfing, checking emails, and logging into AirNote. Checking my university email account first, I see nothing but university announcements. I rarely pay attention to those, because more often than not I could care less what was in them. Logging into AirNote, the first thing I notice is that I have a few new friend requests and a message. Most of the friend requests appear to be from people I met tonight in the choir. Deciding to accept all the friend requests, I start to read the lone unopened message that actually happens to be from Bryan.

Bryan A: Hey there sir! Just wanted to say that it was nice meeting you tonight. You seem like you're cool people. Make sure you come back to rehearsal next week. In the meantime, don't be a stranger.

This message is a little overly friendly, but I guess there is no harm in replying.

Tristan Steele: Nice to meet you too. I had a great time tonight, and plan on being there next Sunday. Have a good one!

Before I can turn on my TV and see what's on for the night, I get another message from Bryan.

Bryan A: Ok cool. By the way, what kind of workouts do you do? I noticed you have a nice chest, and wondering if you could give me some tips.

It's not until reading this, that I'm able to make sense of the "peculiarity" I felt when he and I shook hands. I'm pretty certain that Bryan is gay, and he is flirting with me. I never had someone of the same sex flirt with me before. While I don't agree with the homosexual lifestyle because I was raised to believe it contradicts Christianity, I will never judge or mistreat anyone who is gay. Assuming I know what I know, part of me feels like I should respond by politely rebuffing

Bryan, and ending the conversation. I don't want to mislead him into thinking I'm interested. On the other hand, part of me is flattered with the attention. With two conflicting feelings, I come up with something that embodies both sentiments to a degree.

> *Tristan Steele: Thanks Bryan, I appreciate that. I just do some bench pressing twice a week. Glad my workouts aren't in vain, and someone noticed. Just find yourself a workout routine.*

With one stroke of the "enter" key on my laptop, the message is sent. After reading my outgoing message again, I'm contemplating whether or not it is perhaps a little too bubbly, and not enough "thank you, but no thank you, I don't swing that way."

Bryan A: Oh word! Why don't you let me workout with you sometime. It will be fun ;-)

My last outgoing message was evidently too heavy on the flirty side. Within a matter of minutes, I find myself in unfamiliar territory. I have inadvertently flirted with this guy that found me attractive. The weird thing is, I nearly suffer from panic attacks knowingly flirting with the opposite sex; and yet, my "flirtation" with the same sex came with such ease. It's almost as if my flirting with the latter was instinctive.

However, flirting with a guy is wrong, and I know it. Homosexuality betrays my sense of religion. Plus, it's socially unacceptable among my family, and especially among my best friends from back home. In an effort to pump the breaks on this conversation, I have to make it clear to Bryan what's what.

> *Tristan Steele: So Bryan while I appreciate the compliment, I'm not gay. But hey, I'll see you next Sunday in the choir room.*

Bryan A: Okay cool. I'll see you then.

    I can't tell with that response if Bryan is upset or not, but I know I've done the right thing. After all, I don't like men in that way, and I won't have anyone believing otherwise. I'm straight. Just because I'm flattered by Bryan's attention means nothing. And no matter what's instinctive, I know who I am.

May 18, 2007 (Friday)

"Can you believe we finished our first year in college already," Denise asks as she wheels her suitcase out of her room and into the hallway. "In spite of all the all-nighters, boring classes, and massive amount of homework, we made it!"

"Oh I hear ya," I tell her. "We earned our right to be sophomores."

"Riggggghhhht," she exclaims. "And now it's summertime baby, and I'm so ready! It will be a little weird not seeing you for three whole months though."

"Well, summer will blow by fast, watch," I advise. "And I guess I should expect you to be knocking on my door next semester, seeing that you're moving into the same building I am in the fall. Stalk much?"

While I'm grinning, Denise is shooting me a dirty look and smirking. Even though I told her this as a joke, deep down inside I'm actually excited to have my college bff living near me again this August. The fact Carter would be my roommate again in August too, makes me feel like sophomore year has some great potential.

****

After carrying Denise's luggage to her parent's car, we say our goodbyes, and I start walking to my car to head home to Manassas. On my mini-hike to the freshman parking lot, I think about how the spring semester went by rather quickly. Ironically, my second semester felt like the true start of my collegiate years. I'm a part of the Hamilton fabric now that I'm more than just a student and got involved. And starting next semester, I will be more than an involved student, I will be a student leader.

About two weeks ago before final exams, both BSAS and the Blessed Voices of Triumph held elections for 2007-2008 officers. I'm still shocked I was even nominated for a position in either organization. After all, there were more senior members within each group. However, since joining these organizations I've attended every meeting or rehearsal, volunteered to help out with various fundraising opportunities, and contributed my time and efforts to planning events for the Hamilton community. So I guess my hard work didn't go unnoticed.

Still on my way to my car, I contemplate my quest to become a man of Alpha Ep. Unfortunately, or perhaps fortunately, I've been rethinking this particular goal. When I went to the community service project Bradley invited me to earlier in the semester, I found myself quite disappointed. For starters, most of the chapter of the fraternity was very late arriving to the church where the service project was held. To make matters worse, the brothers didn't really lift a finger to assist with the project once they got there. Instead, they stood around talking about some party they planned to attend later that evening. They made all of us who weren't Alpha Eps do all the work. I guess I wouldn't have been so bothered by their tardiness, had they at least pretended to be more engaged in the actual service that occurred. Ever since that day, I've been more than a little turned off from joining any brotherhood.

Finally approaching the freshman parking lot, I see Chance walking toward me. Since he's a sophomore going on junior, I'm surprised to see him in this lot.

"Hey Chance, how are you?" I ask. "And what are you doing parked over here?"

"I'm good," he replies. "I'm going to work, and oddly enough, this parking lot is the closest to my office. Or should I say our office?"

Partly thanks to Chance, I acquired a job on campus with Hamilton University's Office of Admissions. I am going to be a client services representative, working with other students. My responsibilities will include answering office phones, responding to emails, giving tours to prospective students and major university donors, and various other duties assigned to me. I still feel honored to have landed this gig. This office only staffs twelve students at a time. Considering there are about 28,000 students enrolled at this school, I feel thankful to be a "chosen" one.

"I guess you can call it our office," I chuckle. "Thanks again for putting in a good word for me. I definitely appreciate it."

"No thanks necessary," he states. "I'm actually running a little late, so I'll see you in the office next week right?"

"Yeah," I answer. "Don't let me hold you up, I'll see you next week at work." With that, Chance briskly walks to the office, and I finally hop in my car. Now that my first year of college is behind me, and I have a job to start in a few days, my summer has officially begun.

May 21, 2007 (Monday)

Today is the day that I begin working for the Office of Admissions, and I'm excited, yet slightly anxious. For some reason I keep thinking of all the things that could possibly go wrong on my first day of work. What if I screw up on some important emails? Or what if I enrage a prospective student or parent on the phone? Or in person? Worse yet, what if I do something to piss off my new boss? Despite my fears, I "man up" and make my way to the client services section of the office.

Surprisingly, there is a lot of space back here. I count eight workstations, each equipped with a small desk, a desktop computer, an office phone, and a typical office chair with red padding. Separating each station is a partition that only comes up as far as each computer monitor. As I continue to look around the room, I see my student supervisor sitting at the big workstation in the corner.

"Good morning Stephanie," I say. Stephanie Schaffer is a tall woman originally from Belgium. She is very pale with fire red hair and piercing green eyes. From the first time we met during my interview, I could tell she was extremely professional and sharp as a whip.

"Why hello there," she responds. "I see you believe in getting to work early. You got here before your coworkers." Stephanie is right about me getting to work early. My shift doesn't technically start until 8:00am, and it is currently only 7:45. It wasn't my goal to get here this early, but today is my first time commuting to Hamilton from Manassas during the rush hour traffic. Not knowing how long a usual forty-five minute commute would take this morning, I left home around 6:45am.

"Well it's better to be early than late," I tell her with a fake awkward smile on my face. It's the same smile I displayed during my job interview.

"Indeed it is Tristan," she agrees with a smile of her own. As the head student in charge, she has to be in the office early to unlock the doors, turn on the phones, prepare workload for student employees, as well as log in employees' hours from the prior workday. "So since you're here early, do you want to set yourself up at one of the workstations?"

"Okay sure Stephanie. Does it matter where I sit?"

"No, not at all," she replies. I sit at a workstation in an opposite corner next to the communal refrigerator. It feels like a good location. I'm close enough to Stephanie where I could ask questions throughout the day if I need to. Yet, it's far enough to where I don't have to sit right up under my boss all day. Now if I could only find a drawer at this desk to put my book bag in.

"I see you're settling in," Stephanie says as she stands up from her chair. "We have a few minutes before eight o'clock rolls around, so I'm going to run down stairs and get some coffee. You're more than welcome to join me, or you can hang out here and familiarize yourself with your employee manual."

"Thanks for the offer Stephanie, but I'll just hang here." I ate an egg white breakfast sandwich during the ride here, and I loathe the taste of coffee. Once Stephanie walks out, I pull up a web browser on my computer so I could check to see if my final semester grades are available. I'm pretty sure I did alright on most of my finals, but that biology exam was a pain in the ass to study for. Thankfully, I guess the studying paid off, because it looks like I finished the semester with an A- average. I want to break out into a mini celebration and praise break, but I hear the laughter of two people quickly approaching.

As the giggling draws nearer, I turn around in the chair and spot Chance with Mercedes. I don't really know the girl, but I know of her. She is a short and petite light skin girl, who started as a freshman with me last fall. Plus, she just became a member of Rho Nu Theta Sorority.

"Chance, who is this little boy?" Mercedes scoffs with an "around the way girl" attitude. I'm slightly disturbed by her brash demeanor in the office. And who is she to ask about me like that? Especially knowing I could hear her.

"Now Mercedes, don't do that," Chance interjects. "This is Tristan, he's cool people. Today is his first day working here, so give him a break."

"Alright Chance," she mumbles. "Well Tristan, I'm Mercedes. I see you made yourself at home at my desk." She's staring at me as if she expects me to gather my things and move to another one.

"Oh is it?" I ask. "I wasn't aware that any of the desks had been assigned." Regardless of any expectation Mercedes has of me moving, I have no intention of going anywhere. Stephanie was quite clear that I could sit anywhere, so that's exactly what I'm doing. I mean this is shared space. There simply are not enough computers for every employee to have his or her own desk. It's like a cashier trying to lay claim to a particular register when there are eight cashiers and 3 registers in the store. The only desk off limits is probably Stephanie's.

"Go ahead and sit there today, but know that in the future you need to find another seat," Mercedes cautions.

"In the future, you need to get here before I do," I quip. Displaying a devious grin, Mercedes makes her way to an available desk.

"Don't mind Mercedes," Chance whispers to me. "She is a good person when you get to know her, just a little foolish. You guys will probably become friends." She may be a good person, but I can't see us ever becoming friends.

"Ah Tristan, I see you've met Mercedes," Stephanie says as she reenters through the door. "And of course you already know Chance. Give me a second, and I'll be right over to give you a brief overview of our computer programs."

****

Now that it's four o'clock, I'm glad to be leaving the office. In the course of this day, I think I have learned everything there is to know about university admissions. And in between training, I met three of my other coworkers. Besides Stephanie and I, the rest of the student employees were working part-time over the summer break. They were really only up here to take summer classes and decided to work part-time to earn some extra cash. I have no interest in taking any classes during these three months off. I'm just interested in earning some money so I can stop being so dependent on my mom. I don't want to be that "scrub" that TLC talks about.

"Have a good one Tristan," Stephanie calls out.

"You to," I reply. I scoop up my book bag and head to the exit. Everyone else has already left for the evening, including Chance and Mercedes. I'm not actually thrilled I have to deal with Mercedes while I work here, but I'll have to find a way to manage. After all, I want the dollars and this job makes sense. Pretty good pay, and right on campus. Which will be convenient when the new semester starts. I refuse to allow anyone to ruin this for me, especially this girl and her obnoxious mouth. She may have the outer beauty of a Mercedes, but right now she has all the appeal of a rusted pickup.

July 21, 2007 (Saturday)

    Alex is officially turning nineteen today, and the Manassas crew and I are taking him to Kings Dominion down in Richmond. Although I have not been to the amusement park in years, from what I remember, I always had a good time. Actually looking forward to seeing what new rides they have there. Despite my fear of heights, I really love roller coasters. Growing up trying to explain that to friends and relatives was always a challenge. They couldn't understand, that it's one thing to go up and over a ninety yard hump when you are going one hundred miles per hour. And it's another to sit in a passenger car at the top of a Ferris wheel ninety yards in the air, just dangling there while operators let passengers off at the bottom.

    Now for this particular outing, I somehow got elected to be the driver for the day. As a result, I'm up this morning cleaning out my car. And I mean *clean*. I'm planning to wash and vacuum the car, and take out all the clothes and shoes in it that make it look like an extra closet. In addition, as much as it pains me, I have to throw my beloved Beyoncé in the trunk. I have an image to maintain with the fellas, and her blasting through my speakers when I pick up the crew won't help with that. I wonder if that T.I. CD is in here.

***

    After enduring two hours of heavy traffic to get to Richmond, we finally make to Kings Dominion.

    "Alright, what should we ride first?" I ask my friends.

    "Man, no homo," Alex chuckles. Isaac and Darius are also laughing. As immature as the phrase "no homo" is, we still say it among my group of friends. We use the term when one of us says something that could be construed as a homoerotic innuendo. I've never been particularly fond of the expression, because I hate having to overthink and over analyze everything that comes out of my mouth. Plus, Denise and I had a conversation about how offensive the saying is to those that identify as homosexual. It is like a group of white people going around saying "no black." Even though I know all of the reasons why I should stop participating in this juvenile pastime, I find myself succumbing to the peer pressure when around my friends. I'm already a virgin, and I don't want to further differentiate myself from individuals I've known since sixth grade.

"Shut up," I respond. "What roller coaster should we get in line for first?"

"Ay, let's go get in line behind them," Darius suggests as he gawks at a gorgeous group of girls. The one on the far left is a tall light skin girl, wearing a white tank top and blue jean shorts that hug her mid-thigh. Standing in the middle of the three is this short Latina girl with long and wavy black hair, dressed in similar clothes as her friend (except her tank top was baby blue). Last but not least is this girl on the right. In my opinion, she is the best looking of the bunch. She is about average height for a girl, and has a complexion reminiscent of mahogany wood. Her hair is pulled back into a ponytail that graces her left shoulder. Unlike her other two friends, she is wearing long tight white pants and a black t-shirt that accentuates every curve of her chest.

"Yeah what Duck said," Isaac seconds. With the informal notion having been put before the group, and then seconded, we all follow Darius to get in line behind the girls. They happen to be standing in line for one of the newer rides at the park. Getting closer to the girls, it's a little up in the air who would theoretically pursue which girl. Alex doesn't factor into this equation, since he now has a girlfriend. Isaac broke up with his girlfriend about two months ago, so he's been single and ready.

"Yo I got the tall one," Darius claims.

"Fine with me, I want the girl in them white pants," Isaac asserts. "Baby girl is fine. Tristan you bag that other one." Geez, they could have at least asked who I wanted a shot with. Well I guess it's go time, now that they have a plan.

"So what's going on ladies?" Isaac asks in a somewhat joking manner. He has his infamous Kool-Aid smile on his face, displaying all his teeth. Fortunately for him, most ladies adore this smile. This group of ladies in particular seems to be receptive to his greeting: well, two out of three of them at least. The two females in similar ensembles are grinning from ear to ear, but, the prettiest one has this nasty scowl on her face.

"Um, we are waiting to get on this ride just like you are," this bombshell states with an off-putting attitude and unwelcoming side eye. Her attitude reminds me of Mercedes slightly.

"Whoa little mama," Darius defensively interjects. "No need for the attitude. It was just a question, chill." This comment seems to further alienate her, and cause her friends to start scowling.

"And no need for you to talk to us either," this girl quickly quips. It's funny witnessing this exchange. I know I'm naturally awkward when it comes to flirting with girls, but I don't think I repulse them as Darius just did. Maybe I'll practice my flirting skills, since we are probably going to strike out with these girls anyway.

"Hey Darius, relax for a minute," I interrupt. "She obviously has been hit on several times today, and is really just trying to hang out with her friends and ride these rides." I turn from Darius to face the females, specifically the one with the sour attitude. "Look, we meant no disrespect. We just thought y'all were gorgeous, and were hoping for a chance to talk to you and see if your inner beauty matches what we see on the outside." I'm not sure if that is a good pick-up line given the situation, but it's the one I went with. Looking at the girls, I notice the oddest thing. The girl who just bit my friends' heads off actually looks a little amused.

"Oh thanks," she replies with a little less aggression than she displayed before. "I know you probably think I'm a raging bitch on the inside, but it's just so hot out here, and wack guys have been stepping to us all day being disrespectful." To her point, it is like 99 degrees out here, and heat has a way of making the nicest person irritable.

"I'm Nicole, and these are my friends Chanel and Lisa," she continues. Chanel is the taller friend, and Lisa is the girl that was assigned to me. Now that the ice is broken, perhaps we could actually commence to having a real conversation with these ladies.

****

Leaving the amusement park, all I can think of is how tired I am. My friends and I must have walked every inch of Kings Dominion, bouncing in one line after the next, riding what we could stand to wait for with our new female associates.

"T-man, I still can't believe you got us in with those girls today," Isaac says.

"Yeah, who would have thought that out of all of us, the forty year old virgin would be the one to bag the hoes," Darius snidely remarks.

"The fact that you still think of girls as hoes, may be why you almost blew it with them," I fire back. "Thanks to me, you got a number from Chanel. So I think you meant to say thank you." Isaac and Alex erupt into laughter, while

Darius nods and grins. Despite his jealousy, he can't deny that I'm the reason he is walking away with ten digits this evening. In addition, Isaac was able to get Lisa's phone number because of my efforts. Although Isaac originally expressed interest in Nicole, Nicole was feeling me; hence, me actually getting her contact info.

"Man, can y'all just chill," Alex requests, still chuckling from my comment. "Some of y'all at least got numbers. All I got were a few text messages from an angry girlfriend. Happy birthday to me!"

Sophomore Year

Chapter 3: Fall 2007

August 27, 2007 (Monday)

The official start of my sophomore year in college is today. Unlike the fall semester of my freshman year, I'm actually excited about the start of classes this go around. I'm entering this year having gotten use to campus life and college as a whole. I am a real part of the Hamilton fabric. On the academic side of things, I think I got into a rhythm and knew how much time to dedicate to my studies in order to be successful. In terms of extracurricular activities, I'm going into the school year as the newly elect public relations chair of BSAS and the secretary of Bless Voices of Triumph. In addition, I'm still an employee with the Office of Admissions.

Speaking of work, that's the first thing on my agenda for the day. I'm scheduled to work in the office from nine to one, then I have to head to my Introduction to Criminology class, followed by the course I'm excited about the most this semester, Sociology of Deviant Behavior. I've always been interested in studying what community factors sway one to commit acts of crime, so I figured this course is a must.

"Hey, what time is it?" Carter mumbles as he yawns.

"Oh good morning," I reply. "It's about 8:30. Sorry if I woke you up." I just moved into our new dorm room yesterday and haven't quite unpacked everything. As a result, I am tripping over my stuff piled on my side of the room. My attempt to get dressed as quietly as possible so I wouldn't disturb Carter is failing miserably. On top of that, I can't find my wallet or keys.

"It's okay," he grumbles before rolling over to fall back asleep. After rearranging a few things, I'm finally able to finish getting dressed for work, and even locate what I was looking for. With a wallet and keys in hand, and a book bag on my back, I leave my room and head to work. Even with spending a little extra time searching for my things in the room, I thankfully still have time to stop by the campus coffee shop for a cup of caffeine before my shift at work starts. Since working in the admissions office, I've come to appreciate the hit of caffeine.

****

"Look who's selfish," Mercedes scoffs as I walk to a desk in the office. Ever since our first meeting, she has made a point of getting into the office before me so she could reclaim her workstation. So, I usually work at the desk right next to her. "You couldn't get me anything?"

"Mercedes, you told me you don't drink coffee," I mock while smiling. The craziest thing happened over the summer while working with her. We sort of became friends. Although our initial encounter was less than positive, I actually grew to like her. I've gotten to know the person behind the somewhat rigid exterior. Mercedes is extremely funny, and has a very big heart.

"I mean you could have sent a text to see if I wanted a bagel or something," she jokes as she turns around in her seat.

"Hey Mercedes and Tristan," Chance greets, walking into the office.

"What's going on Chance?" I ask.

"Not much," Chance begins. "I'm just ready to get through this week. It's going to be a crazy one for me. I have something to do every day this week, not including work and school. Actually, what are you doing on Wednesday night?"

"Um nothing besides homework probably. Why what's up?"

"Well you know that I'm now a member of Beta Kappa Nu Fraternity, and my chapter Mu Theta is having a study hall at eight in The Harrison Dean Student Center, Room C. You should come out and see what my fraternity is all about."

Chance became a Beta Kappa Nu man this past spring semester. Unfortunately, I missed his probate show because I was studying for a test with Denise. His membership into the organization was interesting, because apparently he reactivated the fraternity's chapter at Hamilton. The chapter had been suspended by the university for allegations of hazing; although, no official criminal proceedings ever occurred. During the six weeks Chance was working in the office in the summer, he talked with me about fraternities in general, and about his own.

"Okay I'll try to make it out man, thanks," I reply.

"Oh so y'all just gonna talk and not work in here today," Mercedes snidely remarks. "And Chance you know damn well no one that goes to school here calls the student center by its full name. Your bougie behind could have said the HD like the rest of us." Luckily it is only us three in the office right now.

"Mercedes, calm down and stop hollering in here," Chance retorts. "Ain't but a few of us in here." He's pointing to the outside of his hand.

"Then stop all that talking and get to work," she barks, with the slightest of smirks.

August 29, 2007 (Wednesday)

"Where we going for dinner?" Denise questions as we both stand outside of the admissions office. She came to meet me here after I got off, so we could grab a bite before I went to this Beta Kappa Nu thing.

"Hmm, I shouldn't eat anything that would prevent me from being able to stay for the whole study hall if you know what I mean," I joke. I can tell Denise doesn't want to laugh at my slightly crude joke, but she can't help herself.

"Let's just go to the Hamilton Deli," she recommends. The Hamilton Deli was like our campus version of Subway. Except the bread wasn't quite as fresh, and there were no cookies.

"Okay bet, let's go then," I agree.

****

After Denise and I get our subs, we find a seat on the bottom of the HD.

"I still can't believe you're going to this study hall tonight," she says. "I thought you were determined to be Mr. Alpha Ep?

"Denise, it's just meeting a few people and reading a book for one of my classes," I chuckle. "It's not like I'm signing anything."

"Well since you are kind of test driving fraternities now, why don't you…"

"Let me just stop you there," I interrupt. "I will not be looking into Kappa Nu Omega, so you better find another way to get to Ben Watkins." We both erupt into laughter.

"On an unrelated note, what happened with that girl you told me you met at Kings Dominion?" Denise inquires. I told her about Nicole during one of our many phone calls over the summer.

"Essentially nothing," I answer. "We spoke on the phone twice before I figured out she was a little dry and boring. It felt like pulling teeth when I talked to her. So after that second phone call, I didn't call her anymore. A few weeks after that she sent a text to me asking what was up, and I sent her a short generic reply."

"You should have just told her straight up you weren't interested in pursuing anything with her," Denise states, as if I should have known better.

"She's a pretty girl, I figured she would be alright," I mumble.

"Ugh, men," she grunts while rolling her eyes.

****

Having parted ways with Denise and now approaching Room C, I can see through the windows of the space that there are about eleven guys in here. It is set up somewhat like a classroom, and Chance is sitting behind the lone desk in the front. He has on a navy blue t-shirt with the Greek letters B, K, and N embroidered in orange and outlined in white on the front of it. Standing around him are three guys who look older than the traditional young undergrad. I can't tell who the rest of the guys in the room are, as I can only view the back of their heads from my angle.

"Come on in Tristan, and have a seat," Chance instructs as I enter the room. I locate a seat next to the wall, and start heading to it. Walking past the other guys seated at the desks in front of Chance, I recognize most of them as students I've seen on campus, but don't know them personally.

Having sat down, I reach in my book bag to pull out one of my criminology textbooks and a notebook. I have a quiz next week, so I may as well get a jump on studying by reading a few chapters and taking a few notes now. Before I can really start anything however, Chance loudly clears his throat to get everyone's attention.

"Good evening fellas," he starts. "I just want to thank you all for coming out to the first study hall of the year for the Mu Theta chapter of Beta Kappa Nu Fraternity. As most of you know, I'm Chance and I became a proud member of this fraternity this past spring semester. Outside of Beta Kappa Nu, I'm a psychology major, now lead director of the Blessed Voices of Triumph here on campus, a member of the Black Student Awareness Society, a peer diversity counselor, and I work in Hamilton's admission's office. Now the men standing behind me are my older frat brothers, and past members of the Mu Theta chapter. I'll let them introduce themselves."

"What's going on gentlemen?" says the man behind Chance on the left. He is a tall, thin, and light skin man wearing a white button up shirt, grey dress pants, and black shoes. I assume he just came here after getting off of work. Taking a guess, I would say he is in his mid to late 20s. "My name is Gavin, and I crossed Beta Kappa Nu in the spring of 2001. I graduated from Hamilton in 2002 with a B.A. in marketing." The man standing next to Gavin is now grinning and preparing to speak.

"You all will have to excuse my dear brother Gavin here," the man with the grin states. "For those of you who don't know what it means to cross, cross refers to when someone becomes a member of a Greek organization." I knew what Gavin meant, but I guess there could be people in the room who were unfamiliar with the term.

"Well thank you Google," Gavin jabs.

"Gavin, people could have been lost," the man next to him laughs. "Anyways, I'm Arlen and I crossed with Gavin in the spring of 2001, which makes him my line brother. I graduated from Hamilton in 2003 with a B.A. in public affairs." Now Arlen is a little shorter and heavier than Gavin, and has a dark complexion. He too appears to be wearing clothes that signify he came here after leaving work.

The only man left behind Chance to introduce himself is a man about my height. He has a dark complexion similar to Arlen. Although he too appears to just have gotten off work, he managed to have a very *GQ* essence about him.

"Evening fellas," this man states with a certain swagger that just commands attention. "I'm Marcus, and I crossed a year before these two in the spring of 2000. I graduated from Hamilton in 2002 with a degree in business administration. And you young bucks forgive my two brothers. Sometimes they don't know when to just chill." With Marcus rounding out the introductions of the men in the front of the room, Chance looks to the rest of us.

"Now that you all know more about me and some of Beta brothers, I want to go around the room and have you each introduce yourself," Chance requests. I can't believe I have to do yet another one of these "get to know you" activities. At least I don't have to go first I suppose. Chance gestures to the boy sitting on the opposite side of the room to kick off this round of intros.

"Well I'm David," begins the boy. "I'm a sophomore from Ashburn, Virginia, majoring in public relations." David is definitely a familiar face to me, because we shared an English course last semester, and I've seen him in passing from time to time. We have never really spoken to one another, but just acknowledged each other's presence every now and then with a head nod. If I have to guess, his light brown slender build is around six feet.

"Hey everyone, I'm Randy" says the guy sitting next to David. "I'm actually from Durham, North Carolina, and I'm majoring in communications." I have never talked to Randy, but I think he and David are best friends or something. Since freshman year, I've always seen those two around campus together. Although Randy is David's height, Randy has a much darker complexion.

"Before you guys continue introducing yourselves, make sure you guys say what else you're involved in besides taking classes at Hamilton," Chance interjects. "Let us know if you work or participate in any student organizations."

"Oh in that case, I work for Hamilton's Events Management Office, and I'm a cohost of a radio show here on campus," David asserts.

"I'm actually David's cohost on the radio show," Randy adds. Although I don't listen to campus radio, I do remember Mercedes saying something about their show once. I'm pretty sure she said she likes it.

Next to Randy is a short and stocky dark skin fellow. "Ay, what's goin on, I'm Willie," he announces. "I'm an accounting major from Glen Allen, Virginia. It's this small town down by Richmond. I work in the Powerhouse gym, and spend a lot of time there lifting." Willie's job and his extracurricular activity definitely explain his physique.

"So I guess it's my turn," the collegiate sitting next to Willie states in a low voice paired with a hint of an accent. I haven't seen him before, and he sounds as if he could be from somewhere in the West Indies. Looking at him sitting down, he appears to be of average height and body build. He has caramel skin and tightly twisted locks that fall just above his shoulder. "My name's Lamont, and I'm from The Bahamas. Right now I'm working on two degrees, one in computer science and the other in information technology. I'm a R.A. in the junior apartments, I have an internship with Hewlett-Packard in downtown D.C., and tutor on the weekends."

With such an introduction, I understand why I never saw Lamont on campus. He is such a busy guy. Observing the facial expression of everyone else in the room, I gather that they are just as impressed as I am with his credentials. I'm glad I don't have to immediately follow his introduction with my own.

There are now three other guys left to introduce themselves before me, according to the order we appear to be following. Since I have to introduce myself soon, I can't help but tune out the room so I could think of yet again what I would say. I should have what I share in these scenarios memorized by now. I mean I've been in enough of them. As the three guys finish up their intros, I part my lips to speak.

"Hello," I greet the room. "I'm Tristan, a sophomore here majoring in Criminology. As far as what I'm involved in outside of classes, I work in the admissions office here on campus, I am the public relations chair of BSAS, and secretary of the Blessed Voices of Triumph."

Upon completing my intro, a very tall man with dark chocolate skin walks in the room. He is quite muscular and has a strong chiseled jawline. If I didn't know any better, I would think he is on the Hamilton basketball team; however, I've seen enough games to be familiar with the team's roster.

"How you doing sir?" Chance asks him walking into the room. "I'm Chance the president of the Mu Theta chapter of Beta Kappa Nu. We were just going around the room introducing ourselves. Tell us about yourself and find a seat."

"Alright," the newcomer responds. "Well first off, my b for being a little late. I just transferred here this semester from Baldwin Locke University in Philadelphia, and I had a hard time finding this room. Oh, and I'm Kendrick."

"Okay cool," Chance says. "Welcome to Hamilton. Are you a sophomore or junior?"

"I'm a junior majoring in psychology," Kendrick answers.

"So am I," Chance interjects. "One last question, you play ball?"

"Naw, not since the 10th grade," Kendrick laughs. By now he has settled into the seat next to me.

"You're so tall, I had to ask," Chance responds. "Seeing that we've all introduced ourselves, I want to again thank each of you for coming out to my chapter's first study hall of the year. Two of the four principles of my great fraternity are educational attainment and social responsibility; and with tonight, I'd like to think I'm upholding both. Well I'm done talking, so you all go ahead and do some homework or whatever."

"Man, how do they expect you to study at these types of things for real?" Kendrick whispers to me. "After a certain number of people are in a room, people are more likely to socialize than study."

"Ha, is that right?" I question.

"Yeah man," he answers. Once he said that, I look around the room and realize he's right. I'm the only person with a book in front of him, and everyone else is conversing. I feel like a huge nerd, and probably look like one too.

"You may have a point," I agree. "It's Kendrick right?" Now I know his name because he just introduced himself, but I am trying to make small talk.

"Yeah it is. And what's your name? I didn't catch it."

"I'm Tristan."

"Okay, Tristan nice to meet you bruh. So you're trying to be a Beta man?"

"Whoa! I didn't say all of that. I'm just here supporting my boy Chance. He invited me, so I came."

"Oh alright," Kendrick says with an expression of disbelief on his face. "Are you telling me part of you is not here because you're interested in joining this fraternity a little? You had to have thought about it." Part of me wants to know why he is so pressed to know if I want to join. Heck, I just met this dude.

"Right now I'm just interested in checking out what's out here," I respond displaying a phony grin. The kind that one gives when he wants a conversation to move along or end. "Not ready to say I'll join anything."

"Let me stop grilling you," Kendrick chuckles. "I'm just trying to see if we could potentially be brothers one day. But in other news, what's what here at Hamilton? Like where do *we* go around here to have fun?" He puts air quotes around the we.

"Um...well," I hesitantly begin. I don't know what to tell him. I knew what he meant by we, but I don't feel qualified to speak for a majority of the black student body here. I know what Denise and I do for fun, but that's us. I'll just tell him some things I know Mercedes and people in BSAS do on the weekend. "Folks usually go to the black fraternity and sorority parties on campus, or go to D.C. to hit up the clubs."

"Cool," Kendrick says while nodding. "I noticed you said people. What do you specifically do for fun?" I'm surprised he's asking about me in particular. The answer I gave him is a good one.

"I've never been to a party on campus, and I haven't gone clubbing before. I usually go to the basketball games with my friend Denise when the season starts. Other than that, I go to the mall, the movies, and to restaurants off campus. Plus, I'm in the Black Student Awareness Society, or BSAS, and the gospel choir. So I also attend whatever events these groups are having."

"You're a pretty chill guy then," he assumes. "I went to a few fraternity parties back at my old school. They were alright. It's just a bunch of guys grinding on girls until the girls sweat out their shirts and perms. Trust me, you're not missing much on that front. But since I'm new in town, you mind showing me around a little?"

"Sure," I respond. Although I thought Kendrick was a little intrusive at first, he seems like he is could be a decent guy. Also, it would be nice if I could make another male friend on campus besides Carter and Chance. "My friend Denise and I are probably going to go eat and then to the movies this weekend to watch *Superbad* if you want to join us. We will prolly leave campus around eight on Friday night."

"That sounds good man," Kendrick says with a hint of relief in his eyes. I assume he's happy I didn't rebuff his request to hang out, and that he now has some weekend plans.

"Do you live on campus?" I inquire.

"Yeah, I live in the older student apartments next to the Performing Arts Center."

"Alright, I'll pick you up outside of your building Friday."

"Works for me Tristan. Thanks again."

****

Just like that, two hours pass and the study hall session is coming to an end. I have done nothing remotely scholarly. However, I'm certainly not the only one.

"Fellas, we are going to wrap this up for the night," Chance announces. "If anyone is interested in performing community service, on Saturday, September 8th at 10:00 am, my fraternity will be going to the City of Alexandria Family Shelter. We will be helping to stock the shelter's children center with new toys, putting food in the pantry, cleaning up the small playground on the property, as well as other things. Oh, and we will be playing kickball with the kids. Just send me an AirNote message or text if you want to go."

"That's what I'm talking about," Kendrick whispers. "A fraternity that actually does community service. I'm gonna have to check that out."

"I may have to do the same," I reply. After my last time volunteering with a fraternity via the Alpha Eps, I'm a little skeptical about all fraternities' commitment to serve. However, I want to try and keep an open mind. Hopefully if I go the Beta Kappa Nu community service project, I won't have the same bad experience.

August 31, 2007 (Friday)

"What time do we have to go and pick up this guy," Denise sighs. She is a little apprehensive about having a special guest star intrude on our weekly Friday night show.

"Denise, don't be that way," I snicker. "You know his name is Kendrick. And don't worry, we will still have a great time."

"Mm hmmm, we better," she giggles. "So you ready to go?" Since Denise lives three floors above me in this dorm, she just came to meet me in my room so we could head to my car together. It's funny that the tables have now turned, and she finds herself waiting on me.

"Almost," I answer. "Let me grab my phone." I pick up my cell off my bed, and we make our way out of here.

Heading to the car, I decide to text Kendrick to let him know I'm on my way to pick him up. I want to make sure he's ready to go by the time I get to his apartment. If Denise and I have to wait on him, I know she will dislike him instantly when they finally meet. Well dislike him more than she already does.

> *Me: What's up Kendrick? It's Tristan. On my way to pick you up. See you in a few.*

Kendrick: Okay bet! I'll meet you out front.

As Denise and I approach my car, it dawns on me that she may not be able to sit in her usual passenger seat. Kendrick is a giant, and it would be quite cramped for him in the back seat of my car.

"Hey Denise, would you mind hopping in back today?" I timidly ask. "Kendrick is pretty huge compared to us."

"First you invite this stranger on our Friday night hangout, and then you demote me to the back seat," Denise laughs. "But it's cool. Just know I'm choosing where we are eating tonight because of this, and I'm choosing the Cheesecake Factory."

"Okay deal," I agree.

****

"Which one is he?" Denise questions as we pull up to the student apartments next to the Performing Arts Center. There are several guys standing outside in front of the building, but Kendrick's height makes it easy for me to spot him.

"He's the tallest guy wearing the blue polo," I answer.

"Tristan," Denise exclaims. "That boy right there is too fine. Why didn't you tell me? Shoot, I would have worn something else."

"Ha, I didn't notice," I reply. I just lied to Denise. I definitely took notice of his looks. However, as a straight guy, that's not something I should have noticed, let alone say aloud. "I'll take your new found excitement as approval of our special guest." I couldn't help but sound and look a little smug.

"Shut up," Denise giggles. "But what's his story? Is he single? What's he like?"

"Denise, calm down! I just met him the other day. The only thing I know is that he is a junior that transferred here from Baldwin Locke University. And he's a psychology major." Kendrick spots us, and we both get quiet as he walks towards the car.

"Ay T, what's goin on?" Kendrick greets as he gets in the front seat.

"Not much," I respond, while wondering why he reduced my name to a single letter. "How are you? Are you getting use to Hamilton?"

"I'm good," he replies. "I'm still trying to figure things out here." Kendrick starts positioning his body to turn slightly to the back seat. Since Denise is sitting behind me, they are able to look at each other. "And you must be Denise. It's nice to meet you; and, thanks for letting me chill with y'all tonight. I don't really know too many people up here yet, so I appreciate it."

"Oh no thanks needed," Denise says. "Glad Tristan and I can help. I hope you have a good time tonight."

"I hope so too," Kendrick says. "But I can't help but feel like a third wheel on your date night or something."

"Whoa," she gasps. "Tristan and I are just friends. He is like a brother, so don't worry about feeling like a third wheel." It's funny that Denise is so quick to correct Kendrick. I think she is trying to make sure he knows she is Team Single.

"That's good to know," he responds. "Well at least I'm not coming in between romance." We all chuckle.

"Speaking of romance, what about you Kendrick?" I inquire. "You got a boo thang?" I don't really care about his love life or anything, but I'm doing a little probing because I know Denise wants the scoop. She herself would never ask.

"Naw man, it's only me," he answers. "Haven't really been searching for a girlfriend right now either." Looking in my rear-view mirror at Denise, I can't tell if she is excited Kendrick doesn't have a girlfriend, or disappointed he is not looking for one. Either way, she now knows his relationship status.

"Welp, we're here," I announce pulling up to the Cheesecake Factory.

"Awesome, I love this place," Kendrick shares. "T, how did you know this is one of my favorite restaurants?"

"Oh trust me I didn't know. Denise picked it."

"Good call Denise," he tells her.

"Thank you," she softly replies. It's hilarious that this girl went from not wanting to like the boy, to wanting to all but say "I do" to him in a matter of thirty minutes.

****

Finally lying in my bed, I can't stop thinking about what a good night I had. Kendrick actually turned out to be a very cool person and quite entertaining. While at dinner, he kept Denise and me cracking up with all these family anecdotes. Also, I found out over dinner that like me, he is an avid watcher of basketball even though he doesn't really play. I have this feeling he will make a great addition to Denise and I's usual duo. Rolling over to check my phone one last time before falling asleep, I notice a text from Kendrick.

Kendrick: Thanks again man for the invite. Next time I'll drive. BTW, have you decided if you're goin to do that Beta community service thing coming up?

Me: No problem. And I'm still thinking about it. But I'll keep you posted.

Kendrick: Ok bet. Night Bruh.

Me: Night

September 8, 2007 (Saturday)

Campus is pretty dead this morning, but I expect as much for 9:30 on a Saturday. I'm standing outside my dorm waiting on Kendrick to pick me up so we can go to this community service project that Beta Kappa Nu is hosting. Over the past week or so, he convinced me to go. Given how tired I feel, this may have been a mistake. Someone is approaching, and can only assume it's him. So no turning back now.

"Hey Kendrick," I say while climbing into his blue SUV. "Nice whip!"

"T, nice to see ya," he welcomes me. "And thanks. I worked hard to buy her. By the way, I'm kind of excited to do this service today. It will give me a chance to really get to know the Beta brothers. And I looked up the City of Alexandria Family Shelter we're headed to, and it's a shelter for single moms and their children. I'm a product of a single mom, and I witnessed firsthand how hard it can be sometimes. So I'm glad to have the opportunity to help out." It's interesting to find out that this is another thing the two of us have in common.

"That's what's up Ken," I reply. I chose to reduce him to Ken since he insists on calling me T. "I'm the product of a single mother too. I've really got to give my all today helping out then. I guess I should be thankful you're so pressed to be a Beta and convinced me to come." We both chuckle.

"Whatever man," Kendrick scoffs with a grin. The more he and I get to know each other, the more I think we will actually become great friends. "T, what kinds of music do you like to listen to?" I assume he's asking because he is reaching for the radio, and he wants to play something I'll approve of.

"I like a few types of music," I tell him. "I have quite an eclectic taste."

"Oh you're going to give me one of those answers," he sighs.

"What do you mean," I ask, a little puzzled.

"I mean you're giving me one of those generic answers Tristan. Instead of listing off your favorite artists, which I know you have because everyone does, you just tell me you have an eclectic taste. I find people who give generic answers about their musical tastes are afraid they will be judged for what they truly like." I'm slightly amazed how insightful Kendrick is. I did give a generic answer to this question for this very reason.

"Okay Ken, what do you like to listen to?" I deflect to him.

"I know what you're trying to do," Kendrick jokes. "But I'll answer your question, even if you won't answer mine. I'm somewhat of a hip hop head, and I'm a fan of Jay Z, Nas, and Lauryn Hill. I also vibe to quite a few R&B artists like Jill Scott, Anthony Hamilton, and India Arie. Lately I've been listening to this album right here though. It may be pop, but I love it." Kendrick presses the CD button on the center console of his car. As the music starts playing, my jaw drops.

"So what you know about this *Good Girl Gone Bad?*" he questions while smiling at me. I can't believe he has a Rihanna album, and is playing it proudly with me in the car. "I know people think a man can't love Rihanna like I do unless he's gay, but I don't care. Hell, I'm grown!"

"If you like it, I love it," I exclaim. "Who am I to judge?" I'm impressed with Kendrick's boldness, and I admire his ability to disregard public opinion.

"Okay T, I ask again. What kinds of music do you like?"

"Alright I'll tell ya," I start. He wore me down and has made me feel comfortable enough, so I guess I should share. "I'm actually a fan of Kanye West. On the R&B side of things, I like Lyfe Jennings and Musiq Soulchild. Also, I enjoy getting my praise on with Kirk Franklin and Tye Tribbett. Not sure why I'm about to tell you this, because I've told no one; but, my favorite musician in the world is Beyoncé, hands down. I love everything about the woman." Upon revealing my secret for the first time, I can do nothing but look straight ahead out of the front window. I'm trying to avoid eye contact with Kendrick. Regardless of me feeling comfortable enough to share my secret, the fact remains that I've never told anyone this.

"Finally I get the truth from the Tristan Steele. Now was that so hard? I actually vibe with all those artists. And you'll be glad to know, I'm not judging you. Welp, let's turn this good CD up." Kendrick begins blasting "Umbrella."

****

"Fellas, thanks for coming," Chance says to Kendrick and me as we enter through the doors of the family shelter. "We're just waiting on a few others before we get started."

"Hey Chance," I respond. Looking around I happen to notice that the only people here were the three Beta brothers I met a few weeks ago, Chance, that guy Lamont, and two employees of the family shelter.

"Sup Chance," Kendrick greets. Kendrick and I then walk around the lobby of the shelter to exchange our salutations with the other familiar faces.

"Good to see you two again," Marcus says to Kendrick and I as we dap him up. "And man, I forgot how big you are." I know he's not talking to me, because I'm a meager 5'9".

"I've got a little height on me," Kendrick replies. Kendrick must be sick of people always commenting on how tall he is. I know I would be.

"Okay," Marcus snickers. Just then, Randy, Willie, and David come through the shelter's doors.

"Well now that everyone is here, let's get started," Chance instructs. "Each of my brothers has been assigned a special task to complete here at the shelter. In addition, my brothers have been given the name of one or two current students. Together, each pairing will complete the given task." This is quite the creative pairing system. It gives us Hamilton students the opportunity to interact with the Beta brothers on a more intimate level. As Chance rattles off the assignments, I learn that I would be working with Marcus helping to stock the children's center with new toys.

"Let's go get started," Marcus suggests.

****

"Ay young blood, let me ask you something," Marcus says. I think Marcus is attempting to continue on with our idle chit-chat. We have already discussed the weather, recent NFL games, his job, and my time at Hamilton as a student, so I'm not sure what's left to discuss.

"Sure," I reply, while trying to put this Hot Wheels Track together.

"Have you thought much about becoming Greek?" he questions.

"Honestly yes, at one point," I answer. "I thought I knew what I wanted to pledge when I got here, but after a little research, I had to rethink that."

"Oh is that right," Marcus asks smugly. "You sound like me when I was in school. When I first came to Hamilton, I had made up my mind that I would be a man of Kappa Nu Omega. Both my dad and uncle are Kappa Nus, and I wanted to carry on the family tradition. However as time passed, I started to question what else was out there. The Kappa Nus at Hamilton back when I was in school were just throwing parties. They never did any community service, and they had the worst GPA on campus. The Hamilton chapter didn't reflect the organization my dad and uncle always bragged about."

"So I started doing some research into other fraternities on campus, and came across Beta Kappa Nu," he continues. "The Mu Theta chapter at Hamilton actually exemplified the fraternity's national principles and motto. Also, the Beta brothers back then were real cool and down to earth. Look, I'm not trying to pressure you into joining my fraternity. You're here helping us out, so I assume you have somewhat of an interest. I just wanted to tell you about my experience, and let you know I can relate. I recommend you continue to look into the different brotherhoods out here. You'll come to know what organization is right for you. Trust your instinct."

I can't believe how candid Marcus is. It's nice to hear his story about how he came to decide on pledging to be a Beta man. His initial experience with Greek life at Hamilton sounds a lot like my own. I also appreciate the fact that we've been talking for a little over an hour in this children's play room, and he has not once shoved Beta Kappa Nu down my throat. It's funny that after all the research I've conducted on different fraternities at Hamilton, it's this one conversation that pushes me to have my "Aha moment."

****

"Man T, I'm beat," Kendrick mumbles as we climb back into his SUV. We are heading back to campus after a long day of service. "You know, having to help stock the food pantry didn't bother me at all. But playing kickball with a bunch of young kids for the rest of our time at the shelter wore me out. Heck, it made me realize I don't want kids anytime soon. Talk about real birth control."

"Ken," I laugh. "Really? Although, I sure could use a nap myself." "And I have to admit, it felt great to give back. Plus, I think I may be ready to officially jump on the Beta bandwagon with you." Now smiling, I look closely at Kendrick, eagerly awaiting his response.

"Finally, you've seen the light," he snickers. He appears to have received a boost from my news. "Well if you are for sure trying to be down with Beta, you need to discretely let Chance know. This is crazy, we're bout to brothers man!"

"I'll let Chance know Ken. But let's take it one step at a time."

September 30, 2007 (Sunday)

"Is this the place?" Kendrick asks me as he pulls his vehicle into an available parking space.

"Yeah I think so," I answer. "6743 Monroe Place, yep that's it. And there is Chance's car." Kendrick and I were both sent texts from Chance yesterday to meet him at this address at 6:00pm sharp. It's about fifteen minutes until six now. From the look of things, the mystery address is to a pretty decent sized townhome. I have not the slightest clue as to why Chance told us to meet him here.

"Alright, well let's go ahead and knock on the door," Kendrick suggests. "If this is the meeting I think it is, it's better to be early than late." We both jump out of his SUV, and walk up to the home. Once at the front door of the townhouse, Kendrick knocks. As the door opens, we're greeted by Marcus.

"Fellas," Marcus welcomes. "Come on in." Entering the home, I realize by the array of family pictures on the wall with Marcus in them, that this mysterious home belongs to him. "Guys, we're actually heading down to the basement." He opens the door to the stair case and leads us downstairs.

"What's going on fellas?" I hear approaching the bottom step. Although I can't see Chance yet, I recognize his voice.

"Not much, how goes it?" Kendrick responds. Arriving in the basement, there's Chance, Arlen, and Gavin sitting on a beige couch in front of a big flat screen TV. In addition, sitting on the floor to the right side of the TV are David and Lamont. Both Kendrick and I went to greet the Beta brothers first before joining David and Lamont on the floor. Being next to the other non-Greeks in the room feels like the logical thing to do.

"You guys go ahead and talk amongst yourselves," Chance suggests. "It's almost six, and I'm waiting on one more person to get here before we go ahead and get started." I wonder if the person he's waiting on is a Beta or a non-Greek. I guess my curiosity will be short lived, because I can hear someone knocking on the door.

"Let me go answer that, I'll be right back," Marcus says running up the flight of steps. Perhaps due to nerves and/or anticipation, Lamont, David, Kendrick, and I are finding it hard to make conversation with one another. I think we all just want confirmation about the true nature of this apparent meeting.

Walking back down the stairs behind Marcus is a light brown guy that appears to be around my height. "How's it going, I'm Brian," he greets the room. He then walks over towards me and sits down. As Brian continues to introduce himself to Kendrick, David, Lamont, and I, we learn that he is a senior majoring in history. This Brian is definitely different from the last Bryan I met at Hamilton.

"So Brian," David starts. "Has anyone ever told you that you look like Romeo from *The Steve Harvey Show*? Now that David has pointed it out, I can't help but think that Brian indeed resembles the actor that played Romeo.

"Yeah I get that a lot," Brian laughs.

"Alright fellas, can I get your attention," Chance requests. The basement becomes silent. "Thanks everyone for coming out, and thank you Marcus for opening up your home to us. The reason we are all here today is because the Mu Theta chapter of Beta Kappa Nu Fraternity is preparing to conduct fall intake. You five guys in front of me have expressed an interest in joining my great fraternal organization, and have met the criteria for membership. Becoming a Beta is both a financial and time commitment. Before I go further, I need to make sure that the five of you are willing to make such commitments to joining." One by one, David, Lamont, Kendrick, Brian, and I reaffirm our interests.

"Now that I know you all are committed to the process of membership, let's talk about what's next," Chance continues. "Wednesday night will officially begin part of your journey. The five of you will be responsible for getting to this house on time each night until this membership process ends. I'll give one of you the time at some point on Wednesday, so I advise you all to exchange numbers if you haven't already. Also, you each need to buy a black t-shirt and grey sweatpants. Make sure that the shirts and the sweats are the same."

"The most important thing to know about this process is that it's a secret," Chance goes on to say. "What we do here at night is not to leave this basement. In fact, no one should even know you're pledging."

As Chance attempts to continue his rundown, Marcus interjects. "You guys also have to make sure you don't share with anyone from the graduate advising chapter what goes on here. You will have official fraternity membership classes with Chance and graduate chapter brothers, and those brothers will try to gauge whether or not you're pledging underground. It's important that you tell them nothing, and act like nothing is going on. Our chapter just came back to Hamilton, and we don't want to get suspended again for perceived hazing. In fact, unless we bring someone around you in this basement or say otherwise, the only people that know what happens here are the people in this room right now. Understood?" My future line brothers and I nod to signify our comprehension.

Hearing more about the steps to becoming a Beta, I'm starting to wonder if I'm making the right decision. I've seen pledging play out in movies like *School Daze* and *Stomp the Yard*. Am I really ready to have people yelling in my face or even putting their hands on me? I'm too prideful of a person to endure such disrespect without reacting.

However, I understand that pledging is a process that I have to go through in order to become a real Beta man. I found out from Kendrick a few weeks ago that while one can just attend the official membership classes to join a predominantly black Greek organization, he wouldn't be considered a real part of the organization until he completed an underground pledge process. Since I already made it known amongst everyone in the room that I'm in this for the long haul, I suppose I won't back out now.

****

"Man T, you ready for all of this?" Kendrick questions as we ride back to campus. I can tell he is excited. "You know I've been ready."

"Yeah, for the most part," I reply with a little apprehension. "Not sure if I'm ready to be treated like some animal though."

"I get that," he responds. "But you'll pull through it. I'll make sure of it. I got your back." I actually feel reassured by Kendrick's supportive words. "Since we only have a few days left of freedom, you want to go to the movies, or go grab some food or something?"

"We might as well," I sigh. "Can we stop by campus and pick up Denise first?" I figure she would like to hang with us off campus. I probably won't get many chances to hang out with her while I pursue Beta.

"Of course T!"

November 1, 2007 (Thursday)

It's about four weeks into my Beta membership process, and I'm beyond exhausted. Trying to balance my time between the admission's office, BSAS, the choir, the pledge process, and classes, I'm just wiped out. I'm operating on about two to three hours of sleep a night. Although I'm trying to keep up my appearance and at least look like I'm not pledging, I'm not sure I'm succeeding. Yesterday at work, Mercedes kept making slick remarks to me. She said things like, "oh, I see someone trying to cross the burning sands," or "word on the street is you're on line." Stuff like this to basically accuse me of trying to become Greek. I just played coy with Mercedes until she stopped.

"Ay T, I'm so glad we don't have to go to Marcus' house tonight," Kendrick exclaims as we enter his student apartment. We just got back from detailing Marcus' car, and are waiting for the rest of our quintet to arrive. Since David, Lamont, Brian, Kendrick and I have the night off from pledging, we decided to meet up at Kendrick's place to study Beta.

"Man me too," I reply. "Last night really got to me though. Arlen kept grilling us about chapter history and that stupid 'Invictus' poem. He knew we definitely didn't have time to memorize that poem perfectly in the hour he told us before meeting up at Marcus' spot."

"Tell me about it," he states in a resentful tone. "It was like he was looking for a reason to give us wood." The term "wood" in this case doesn't necessarily refer to what you throw in a fire. Kendrick is referring to the paddle that is used to "punish" us pledges when we did or said something wrong. Which apparently is all the damn time. None of us like getting hit with the paddle, but Kendrick especially hates it. By now, each of us have all sorts of marks on our butts from the physical reprimanding.

"Right," I chime in.

"T, I was talking to my cousin who pledged Beta at Eastern New Jersey University, and he said using Vaseline helps with the bruising."

"Really?" I ask.

"Yeah T. He said him and his line brothers would rub it on each other's ass after rough nights. Before you ask, they weren't gay." I'm glad he answered the question before I had the chance to ask.

"Um ok," I mumble. I'm not quite sure where this conversation is going.

"Look, I'm just going to ask you this before the rest of the guys get here. Do you mind rubbing some Vaseline on my bruises? T, I feel like we are the closest, and you wouldn't necessarily bug out like David, Lamont, or Brian." I'm completely baffled by his unusual request. I mean, why can't he put Vaseline on his own butt? On one hand, I would feel very uncomfortable rubbing on his body, especially below the waist. On the other hand, if I tell him no I may come off as immature, and make this now uncomfortable situation more awkward. What to do? What to do?

"Uh… I guess I can do it." I'm in sheer disbelief that I agreed to do this. It's like the words just fell out of my mouth. "But Ken, you can't tell anybody what I'm about to do."

"Deal! I appreciate this so much," Kendrick tells me. "You're a real friend and a good brother. I'm going to run to my bathroom and grab the Vaseline. I'll just meet ya in my room." I nervously walk to Kendrick's bedroom. I want to get this over with as quickly as possible. I sit on the chair near his desk, dreading what I agreed to do.

"Here you go T," Kendrick says as he walks in and hands me a jar. He then proceeds pulling down his pants and underwear. As his bottoms drop around his ankles, all I can see are his chiseled thighs and muscular buttocks. His black A-shirt does nothing to hide his tight glutes. Wanting to hurry this along, I locate the bruising on both his left and right cheeks. Despite having a darker complexion, the bruising is still quite visible. While still looking at the marks, I attempt to open the jar of Vaseline. Unfortunately for me, the container is so greasy that I manage to drop it on the floor, and it rolls around to the front of Kendrick's right foot. Perhaps sensing that I don't want to reach around him to get it, Kendrick bent his 6'8" frame over and reaches for the jar. With him bent over, I'm—oddly—unable to look away. His ass is damn near in my face.

With my eyes set on such an unfamiliar view, a peculiar thing begins to occur. Looking down at my sweat pants briefly, I notice that the seat of them is rapidly expanding. I can't make sense of why this is happening right now; I mean I'm not gay. Heck, I've been in locker rooms plenty of times in high school, and this never happened. Regardless of the reason why this is happening, it's happening, and I have to readjust myself before Kendrick peeps it.

"Here you go butter fingers," Kendrick says as he slightly turns his body to give me the jar. Luckily for me, I don't think he spots the situation going on in my *nether regions*. After taking the container and a deep breath, I scoop a glob of Vaseline out with my right index and middle fingers. I spread the petroleum jelly in my hands, and start rubbing it on his bruised posterior. At this moment, I think I would be more comfortable dressed from head to toe in steaks while standing in a cage full of lions.

"Tristan, can I share something with you?" For the life of me, I don't understand why he chooses now to want to share something with me.

"Yep, go ahead," I answer.

"Well, you know how I said I wasn't checking for a girlfriend a while back?"

"I remember Ken. Why?

"Well, I haven't been checking for a girlfriend for a while now, because…because…." He pauses, so do I. "Because, the last relationship I was in ended badly, and I can't seem to move on from them." If this is what he wanted to tell me, I think it could have waited.

"I wouldn't worry about checking for a girlfriend right now anyways," I tell him. "You're young. No need to settle back down. Besides with us on line right now, who has time to date?"

"I guess," Kendrick mutters, sounding unsure or something. "But hey, are you almost done?"

"Sure am. I'm going to use your bathroom real quick to wash my hands." Before I stand up I take an opportunity to shift junior in my underwear, because he's still very much at attention. Trying to conceal my aroused member is proving somewhat difficult. Once I did some shifting, I get up and walk to the bathroom. In this moment, I'm just relieved knowing Kendrick's roommate spent most of his time at his girlfriend's apartment and is rarely here.

****

Although I've been in the bathroom for a good while, I refuse to leave it until all my blood rushes back to where it is supposed to be. To help the process along, I've been thinking

Majoring in Me 82

about pigeons. For some reason these birds give me the creeps, and are definitely a turnoff. Thankfully, this seems to be doing the trick. Finally almost flaccid, I leave the bathroom and attempt to make a beeline to the living room.

"Ay T," Kendrick calls out before I can make it past his bedroom. "What took you so long? I thought you fell in the toilet or something."

"I was just getting myself together, that's all." Is that the best answer I could think of on the spot?

"Well T, do you want me to spread some Vaseline on your bruises?" Now that is something I don't want, because at this point I think my loins have an inexplicable mind of their own and I don't want to risk having another erection. And with my pants down at that.

"Naw Ken, I'm good. But thanks for the offer though." I again attempt to walk to the living room.

"T, you sure? You got a lot of wood yesterday, and I know you've got to be sore. It's just brotherly medical aid damn," he laughs. Going against my better judgment, I veer back into Kendrick's room.

"Alright man, let's just do this," I say unenthusiastically. And again fully clothed, Kendrick eases his way into the desk chair. I hesitantly pull my pants and underwear down with my backside facing him. I don't want to give him a frontal shot. Also, I want one last chance to inspect my parts to make certain everything is still calm. Within a blink of an eye, I'm standing in front of my new Hamilton friend and soon to be Beta brother practically nude.

"I can definitely tell you ran track," Kendrick jokes as he rubs the grease on my now clinched ass. The joke has made me even more uneasy. "Relax T, damn." I guess he took notice of my tension.

"Man sorry, this is just a little weird," I reply. I mean it's hard to relax in such uncharted waters. It's becoming even harder to do so, because the more Kendrick rubs his hands across my cheeks, the more I get aroused all over again. I've got to end this. "I think you got all the bruises Ken." I abruptly bend over and pull up my boxers and sweats. Dressed and about to return to the bathroom, I turn my head slightly to Kendrick to say thank you. However, I witness something strange. I notice his navy blue silk track pants are unsuccessfully concealing what looks to be his largely swollen symbol of manhood. I attempt to quickly turn back around, but our eyes somehow lock on one another. Kendrick has this look of surprise plastered on his face. Before more words could be exchanged between the two of us, we hear a loud knock at his front door.

"One second," Kendrick hollers out.

November 28, 2007 (Thursday)

Although I thought today would never get here, it did. Today David, Lamont, Bryan, Kendrick, and I are finally being revealed to the campus as the newest Beta men of the Mu Theta chapter. The guys and I have been through so much to get to this point. With only an hour left until this big probate show, we are rehearsing and trying to calm our nerves in the basement of Winston Hall. It's one of the older buildings on campus, and people rarely come here after seven.

"I can't believe we made it," David exclaims. "No more people yelling in our faces telling us how wrong we are! No more living off of coffee and energy drinks! And more importantly, no more taking wood!"

"Hell yeah," Lamont hollers. "We bout to bag all these girls on campus too." The room erupts into laughter. However, Kendrick isn't amused.

"Hey Ken, what's up with you?" I ask as I walk over to him.

"Man T, I just got a text from my cousin that's the Beta, and he and my uncle won't make it here for the probate. Apparently, my cousin got held up at work and is just getting off. Considering it's about a three hour drive, they won't get here in time even if they left right now." I know how much Kendrick wants them to see this big moment, so I feel bad for him.

"Sorry to hear that," I reply. "But hey, your mom is here. Plus, Denise will be yelling for you. Not to mention, I've got my friend Alex recording the show, so I'll get you a copy for your fam." I told my best friends from back home about me pledging a few days ago, but Alex is the only one that could make it to tonight's probate.

"T, I really appreciate that. I'll definitely owe you one if you can get me that copy."

"Don't worry about owing me anything. We're brothers." Surprisingly enough, the relationship between Kendrick and I hasn't really changed after the *incident*. Neither one of us has actually brought up what happened that night in his apartment. I haven't told anyone what happened, and I can only assume he's done the same. We both have been acting like nothing ever occurred, and I didn't see what I saw. I think we both know that discussing what transpired could damage our friendship and brotherhood.

Despite the fact Kendrick and I didn't address the issue, I actually thought about it to the point of obsession for a few days after that night. I couldn't stop wondering why I got aroused by Kendrick. I tried to rationalize that my erection stemmed from my novice experience with being that close to the naked human anatomy. Heck, I had never even watched porn before. It's necessary for me to believe this theory, because the alternative one I'm not able to embrace.

In addition to trying to make sense of my own behavior, I've attempted to make sense of Kendrick's behavior. I mean, he had a clear erection as well. In my mind, I can't justify Kendrick's erection with the theory I applied to my own, because Kendrick's been in a relationship before. Naturally I assume he consummated the relationship; and therefore, he is not a stranger to the flesh.

As I think more about it, the more I think that perhaps Kendrick is bisexual or gay. After all, he said he wasn't looking for a girlfriend. And, when he referenced his past relationship, he didn't use a gender specific pronoun. He used the term *them*. However, I don't want to make wild assumptions about my friend. All in all, I find it best to just attempt to forget about the whole ordeal.

****

After forty minutes of my line brothers and me rattling off fraternal history, listing off names from the chapter's lineage, reciting poems and mantras, and performing a little step, it is time for us to individually introduce ourselves. Since I am the shortest of the bunch, I'm up first.

"I am Tristan Steele," I begin shouting with all the intensity I could muster. "I am the unbreakable ace of this line, and have led my brothers to this great moment! I'm a sophomore majoring in criminology, reppin Manassas, Virginia! From this day forward, I will be known as Silent Threat! Y'all wanna know why?" Marcus and the other older brothers had coached me to pose this question, and wait for them to reply *why*.

"Why?"

"Because there are those that have doubted me and my abilities. They underestimated what I was capable of, and never saw me coming. But when they pushed me to my limits, my doubters became believers, and they realized all along that I am the Silent Threat!" Upon completing my individual introduction to the campus, I hear a loud roar of applause and cheers. I spot Denise standing next to my mom. Both beaming with pride.

One by one, my line brothers follow suit and introduce themselves to the campus, going from shortest to tallest. After me is Brian. His fraternal line name is Poker Face. No one could ever read his face to gauge his emotions, which served him well while we were pledging. The big brothers didn't like to see us show anger or frustration during our process, and no one hid such emotions better than he did. So his new fraternal name is quite fitting.

Next to Brian is Lamont. He was given the line name International Hustler, which is so him. Lamont has multiple jobs, and is always looking to add another side hustle to his repertoire to make more money. Before we began pledging, I never understood where he found the time to sleep with all the stuff going on with him. However, once we started our fraternal journey, I soon learned coffee is his drug of choice, and sleep to him is more of a luxury than necessity.

On the other side of Lamont, is David. Out of all my line brothers, he is without question the most popular one. When he introduces himself to the Hamilton community, the crowd goes crazy. The big brothers named him Smooth Criminal. His line name is a reflection of his Michael Jackson-like ability to dance. David's dancing skills came in handy when my line brothers and I had to entertain our big brothers during one of our many nights in Marcus' basement. The dancing talent also benefited us in putting together this entertaining display of showmanship tonight.

Last, but certainly not least, is Kendrick. Kendrick appropriately received the name The Muscle. The older brothers gave Kendrick this name because he was so protective of me and my line brothers during our nightly encounters with wood. He was especially protective of me. In addition, Kendrick's new given name describes his stature. As the tallest person of the five of us, and rippling in defined pecs, lats, tris, and bis, he is indeed The Muscle.

Concluding all of the introductions, members of the crowd in attendance rush us, offering various congratulatory words, balloons, and gifts. Making my way through the crowd, I hurry over to hug my mom and thank her for coming. It's a weeknight, and I know she has to get to bed soon because she has to work in the morning.

"Great job Tristan," my mom claims. "I'm so proud of you. I'm going to ask you one more time though, did they hit you?" She asked this question a few times before, but I lied to her and told her no one laid a finger on me. Because she is my mom, deep down inside I think she knows I had been hazed to some degree.

"Ha," I nervously laugh. "I already told you Mom, no one hit me."

"Mmhmm," she grumbles. "They better not have touched my baby. Well, I'm going to get out of here and let you celebrate with your friends. I love you, and I'll talk to you later. And be careful!"

"Thanks again for coming Mom. I love you too, and text me when you get home." We hug one last time, and she makes her way to her car. I take a few steps to the right to celebrate with my sister from another mister, Denise.

"If it isn't Mr. Silent Threat," Denise giggles. "Tristan I'm so proud of you. You looked really good out there. I can't believe my college bestie was out there getting it!"

"Thanks Denise," I smile. "Everybody is trying to go celebrate at Chili's, you want to go?"

"Naw Tristan," she answers. "I think I'll sit this one out. But you go ahead and celebrate with your brothers. Truth be told, I'm tired. All I want to do is crawl into my bed.

"I hear ya," I say. "I secretly want to crawl under my own covers. It's been a minute since I've had some real sleep."

"Tristan, you'll only experience this night once, so find some energy and go."

"I know, I know," I respond.

"Yeah, you do that Silent Threat. Now let me go find Kendrick and congratulate him so I can get going," Denise hugs me goodbye.

"Thanks again Denise for coming." As she walks off, I immediately feel someone hit me on the back of my left shoulder. Turning around, I see it's Alex.

"Hey what's up?" I say.

"What's up?" he rhetorically questions. "You are the one that just became a Beta. Who knew T-Man could do all that? Do me a favor and remember one thing."

"What's that?" I inquire.

"Remember you had brothers before you had brothers," Alex jokes. "Don't forget about the crew from Manassas."

"Lex, now you know you don't even have to worry about that. You already know y'all are my fam for life. But hey, my frat and I are going to Chili's to celebrate. You want to go?"

"I wish I could T-man, but I'll have to pass. I have an English paper due tomorrow, and out of ten pages I've written three." Alex had enrolled in courses at the local community college in Manassas this fall. His plan is to finish some general education courses there before transferring into Old Dominion University.

"Alright man," I respond. "Appreciate you making out here for the probate at least."

****

It's approaching 1:30 in the morning, and all I want to do is lay my head down on my pillow. After a few hours at

Chili's, I'm officially exhausted and sick of celebrating for the night. Thankfully I'm riding with Kendrick and Brian, and we are heading back to campus. David and Lamont decided to continue celebrating by going over to some girl's apartment. Apparently this girl invited some of her girlfriends to her place, and told me and my line brothers to come over for somewhat of an after party. Lamont and David were the only ones up to go.

"Thanks for the ride Kendrick, aka The Muscle," Brian states as he opens the door to get out of the vehicle. He's the first one to be dropped off since he lives off campus with his girlfriend.

"No problem B," Kendrick replies. "And let's hit that call one more time. "Beeetttaaa," he hollers out.

"Kappa Nu," Brian and I yell in response. We completely disregard the hour of the night and the neighbors in Brian's community. Brian then climbs out of the SUV, closes the back passenger car door, and leaves Kendrick and me alone to drive back to campus.

"We are Betas," Kendrick exhales beaming with pride.

"Yeah man, I'm hype about it too," I exclaim. "We are real legitimate men of Beta Kappa Nu." Just that quickly, Kendrick develops this weird somber expression on his face.

"Hey Tristan, do you mind if we have a real conversation?" Even though I'm not in the mood to have any deep discussion, I can tell he really wants to talk.

"Sure Ken, what's goin on?"

"Well this may not be the right time to talk about this, but it's been on my mind for weeks." Here we are, about to have the very conversation I have been dreading and trying to avoid. Kendrick drives right past my dorm and is pulling into the parking lot behind Winston Hall. "So you remember that night when we here helping each other with our bruises?"

"Yeah I remember," I mumble.

"We never really talked about what you saw. I wanted to have a conversation with you before tonight, but the opportunity never presented itself. Then I told myself I'd wait until we were done pledging before I brought it up; and well, here we are."

"Wait a minute," I interrupt. "We don't have to talk about this."

"Yeah I think we do," he counters. "Look I haven't told a ton of people this yet, but that relationship that I told you I was involved in, was with a man. I'm gay. I'm not on the down low or anything, I'm just discreet. In my opinion, it's not the public's business what I do in private. And people always seem to prejudge you when they find out you like guys. Before I go too far on a tangent, I say all this to say that I like you. I've liked you since the day we met." With this confession, my mind and heart start racing. I've never had a stroke or heart attack before, but I suddenly feel as if I am experiencing both.

"I'm sorry to just pile this on your lap," Kendrick goes on to say. "But I just couldn't hold this in any longer. Tristan, I feel like we have this special connection that extends beyond simple friendship, or even brotherhood. Don't you feel it?" I really want him to stop talking at this point. This conversation is way too much for me to handle right now. Slowly but surely my feelings of anxiety are transforming into anger. I mean, how dare Kendrick put me in this position. And on tonight of all nights. How does he want me to respond?

"Kendrick, what are you doing right now? Why would you choose to tell me this now? Tonight was supposed to be about us professing to the world that we're Beta men. But now, the memory of this night will be tainted by your own personal coming out story. And man while I'm flattered you find me attractive, nothing will ever happen between us because I'm not gay. And did you make up that whole thing about Vaseline helping with bruises just so you could have a reason to touch me? Man, that's sick!"

"Come on Tristan, don't do that! I hope you know me well enough by now, to know I wouldn't sink that low. That treatment was real, and it was between friends and brothers. I didn't suggest us doing that just so I could get off. Besides, if I really wanted something to happen between us that night, I think we both know you would have been down for it. Did you forget you got hard that night too?" I can't believe Kendrick saw my erection. Moreover, I can't believe he just brought it up. Although my natural instinct is telling me to deny that I had an erection that night, I find myself opting to take a different approach.

"Man, I don't care what the hell you think you saw, I'm not gay," I shout. With this proclamation, I could sense the mood shifting to something ugly.

"Hey," he interjects with a little more base in his voice. "I get you say you're not gay, but you need to calm down and lower your voice. Just because I'm gay, doesn't mean you get to talk to me any ole kind of way."

"I can't do this, I'm out," I scoff as I open the car door. Kendrick then yanks my arm.

"T, don't leave like this! Let me take you back to your dorm."

"That's alright, I'd rather walk back. I wanna clear my head. But don't worry Ken, your secret is safe or whatever. See you later!" And with that, I jump out of the SUV and close the door. I hear Kendrick hollering out my name; but, that's not deterring me from making my solo trek back to my room.

December 9, 2007 (Sunday)

    Almost two weeks have gone by since Kendrick and I had our slightly heated exchange in his SUV. We haven't really spoken since that night. He tried to reach out to me via texts, but I was never in a headspace to respond. But now that I've had time to think, I believe I am ready to face him. If there is any hope of Kendrick and I moving forward in brotherhood and friendship, a conversation has to occur. Knowing this, I sent a text to him asking if I can come over to his place to talk. I figured his roommate would probably be at his girlfriend's place, and this discussion calls for privacy. Since he agreed to meet me, I'm heading to his place now.

****

    Still not one hundred percent sure as to what I'm going to say, I softly start knocking on Kendrick's apartment door.

    "Hey Tristan," Kendrick welcomes. "Come on in." As I walk past him in the doorway and enter his apartment, I can tell he is just as nervous as I am about what might be said tonight.

    "How you doin Kendrick?" I ask. "Is your roommate at his girlfriend's again?"

    "I'm good," he replies. "And yep, you know he stays over there." Kendrick then closes his front door, and we head to the campus issued couch in his living room.

    "So Ken, I want to talk about what happened a while back." I decide it's best if I just go ahead and dive right into the deep end so to speak.

    "Yeah I figured," he mutters. "Look I realize that my delivery and timing may not have been the best, and I apologize for that. However, I can't apologize for being gay, and I can't apologize for feeling the way I do about you."

"Well I actually owe you an apology too," I interrupt. "I thought about how hard it must have been to come out to me, and share your feelings. And how poorly I responded. Even if I thought the timing was bad, I shouldn't have been so quick to snap and disrespect you. We're friends and now brothers, so you deserve better." Looking at Kendrick's body language, I sense that he is starting to relax.

"Thanks for the apology T, I appreciate it. Really!"

"No problem Ken. I just have one more thing I have to tell you. While I absolutely view you as a friend and brother, I can't view you or any man in a romantic way. I'm flattered that you find me attractive, but I just can't say the same. I'm sorry." I'm not sure whether or not I'm being completely truthful. After all, I was in fact aroused around Kendrick. But due to my fear of confronting what could be, I make the conscious decision to downplay any uncertainties and move on.

"Oh I see," Kendrick mumbles. I'm positive he's disappointed. But I don't know if his disappointment stems from me not reciprocating his feelings, or from me not having the courage to be honest with myself.

"I hope we can get past this, and go back to being friends," I tell him. I do miss talking to him about any and everything. Also, I miss us just hanging out. Not to mention, I'm getting tired of Denise asking what's going on between Kendrick and I, and why we haven't been hanging out.

"You know what T, I think I'd like that. Thanks for being cool about this. A lot of guys would write me off. It's good to know our friendship isn't ruined."

"All put behind us Ken. So in other news, what do you think this chapter meeting is about tomorrow?"

"Well," he replies. My guess is that we are going to talk about chapter elections and possibly bringing in new members next semester. Regardless, it's our first official meeting we'll attend as Betas." And in a matter of minutes, the two of us begin our transition back to normalcy.

Chapter 4: Spring 2008

February 4, 2008 (Monday)

I'm going to need several cups of coffee and a prayer if I'm going to make it through this day. I have to work from eight to three, attend two back to back classes from 3:30 to 6:15, go to an executive board meeting for BSAS at 6:30, and meet with Denise at eight for dinner. To top it all off, I have a Beta Kappa Nu meeting of sorts at eleven. The meeting with my frat stands to be quite lengthy, given that tonight we are beginning the pledge process for a whole new group of Hamilton guys.

It was at the meeting back in December that we decided as a chapter to welcome new members this spring semester. In addition, at the meeting we elected chapter officers. Based on the results of the election, Chance went from being chapter president to becoming the membership chair. He is now overseeing all things regarding the initiation of new members. As for the rest of us, Kendrick was elected president; Brian, vice president; Lamont, treasurer; David, community service chair; and me, secretary. Although I was elected secretary, I find myself doing more than my position requires. Being secretary for the gospel choir doesn't demand nearly as much energy or time. But I swallow whatever grievances I have about it, all in the name of Beta.

****

"Well look at Mr. Beta," I hear a voice say as I walk to a desk in the admissions office. I know that voice belongs to Mercedes even without seeing her. She's been calling me this since I became Greek. Mr. Beta however, is a much better greeting than "hey boy" or "hey negro." So I welcome the upgrade.

In addition to an upgraded greeting, Mercedes has also been even nicer to me since I became Greek. For example, anytime she goes downstairs to grab breakfast or lunch, she always offers to bring me something back. While to most people this sounds like obvious common courtesy, this wasn't common behavior for Mercedes. She usually expects me to be the offeror, so it's shocking that I've been the offeree. Also, Mercedes speaks with me more frequently outside of the office. By no means am I bothered by this newfound treatment and attention, but I'm curious to know whether it comes from her having gotten to know me better, or my new fraternal affiliation.

"Hey Mercedes, what's goin on," I inquire.

"Not much," she replies. "Here in this office trying to get my money up." We both kind of chuckle.

"So did you make it last night?" I ask Mercedes. Last night we were texting one another and she asked me if I felt like taking a trip to the IHOP near Hamilton. Knowing today would be so busy, I declined her invitation and opted to get some rest instead.

"Naw, I didn't make it because a certain someone flaked, and left me hanging." Mercedes shoots me a glare with a smirk on her face.

"I told you I got you next time girl."

"I may not give you a chance for a next time," she snickers.

****

After an exhausting day, I finally have some down time to take for myself before I have to meet up with my chapter. So I've been sprawled out across my bed. All of a sudden my phone starts to ring. I guess five minutes of uninterrupted rest is better than nothing.

"Hello," I answer trying not to sound too annoyed.

"Hey T," Kendrick responds. "Are you ready for tonight?"

"Yeah Ken. So what's up? I was trying to get a little sleep before we have to go."

"Oh, you did tell me you were going to have a crazy day," he says. "My b for interrupting your nap and what not, but just want to let you know that Marcus' son is now sick, so we won't be able to meet up at his place tonight. Instead, we are meeting up at Gavin's apartment around ten. Since he lives further away from campus than Marcus, I'm trying to leave Hamilton around 9:30." Trying to process what Kendrick is telling me, I pull the phone from my face to check the time, and it shows 9:20. It's official. That five minutes is all I'm going to get right now.

"Okay," I sigh. "Call me when you pull up outside my building."

"Will do T."

****

"Uh, I'm getting hungry," Lamont begins. "Can we ask these young boys to stop at Wendy's or something to get us some food?"

"Lamont, it's the guy's first night," David replies. "Besides, let's focus and finish up this discussion before they get here." My line brothers, Chance, and I have been at Gavin's home for about forty-five minutes now discussing how the pledge process will be conducted for these new guys. Kendrick and I have been rallying in opposition to this new group of pledges being subjected to the physical side of becoming a member of Beta. We don't understand its necessity, and don't want to hit grown men with a paddle. However, the others are currently overruling the two of us, as they are in favor of keeping with "tradition."

"I thought we finished the discussion," Lamont inserts. "We got wood, so these boys will get it too! Most of us agree, so case closed. Now about this Wendy's? Do you all want something or not? I'm hungry and I'm texting them to get me some food." Lamont is apparently ending the conversation about pledging and moving on.

"Heck if Lamont is getting some food, I might as well get some too," Brian chimes in. With that, Chance jumps on the bandwagon as well.

****

Another forty-five minutes have passed, and finally the doorbell rings. Considering what time of night it is, it has to be the new boys. It's crazy to think that I'm about to be on the other side of the pledge process. Now people will be calling me "sir" and "big brother." As amazed as I am by this fact, I refuse to become "neo happy." Kendrick told me that neo happy is a term used to describe Greeks that act cocky because of their apparent new status. He said most folks that are neo happy badly mistreat pledges. I refuse to be labeled as such a thing.

One by one, the three new guys pile into the living room and form a horizontal line from shortest to tallest. The shortest of the bunch is Willie. It's the same Willie that attended the Beta Kappa Nu study hall and community service event last semester. Due to a family emergency, he was unable to join the chapter last semester. But he is available to try his hand at membership this go around.

Next to his stocky body build is James. James is a taller lanky white guy. James didn't attend any of the Beta Kappa Nu events last semester because his girlfriend recently had a baby and he was trying to get used to being a new parent. So last semester if he wasn't in class or at work, he was with his newborn. Chance told the chapter that James has always wanted to become a Beta since they were both freshmen together, but life circumstances always seemed to prevent him from joining. When James assured us that he is ready to balance school, work, fatherhood, and the pledge process this semester, we decided to give him a shot.

On the other side of James is Randy. Randy attended the study hall and community service activity last semester like Willie. Unfortunately for Randy, he didn't meet the GPA requirement to become a Beta last semester. It seems kind of ironic that he went to study hall and failed to get good grades. However, while my line brothers and I were in the midst of the membership process last semester, he made time to actually hit the books so he could pull his grades up. With him, James, and Willie standing in front of us, it's now time to get this thing underway.

"So why in the hell y'all niggas late?" Lamont barks. The new boys look slightly shook by my line brother's demeanor. Right off the bat, I see not all of us here have a fear of being viewed as neo happy.

April 26, 2008 (Saturday)

I'm so freaking anxious. In a few moments, I along with David, Brian, Chance, and Lamont are about to hit the main stage. Tonight is Hamilton's 16th Annual Greek Step Show, and the five of us are stepping on behalf of the Mu Theta chapter. Kendrick elected not to step with us. Unfortunately for him, he has no rhythm whatsoever. He basically defies the stereotype that all black people can dance and keep a beat.

Even though I'm extremely nervous, I am certain that the fellas and I are ready to kill this show. In the midst of the new boys' membership process, our step team spent countless hours practicing the moves Arlen taught us. Heck for weeks now, my hands have been nearly raw from all the clapping.

"Now welcoming to the stage, those brothers of Beta Kappa Nu," the step show host yells. "Good luck fellas!" Once the lights dim, the guys and I sprint out on stage to begin our routine.

It's crazy to think how my nerves have all of a sudden been engulfed by a surge of adrenaline. I'm now front and center on stage. I feel like I'm Michael Jackson or someone. The people in the audience calling out my name just gives the performer within more of a boost. The usually reserved and relatively quiet Tristan disappeared, and this new person has emerged. Like an alter ego.

****

Before I know it, twelve minutes have gone by and the guys and I are making our way back off of the stage. We are all breathing hard as if we'd run a complete marathon. Me in particular, I stepped so hard that not only am I gasping for air, but also I'm sweating profusely. My shirt is soaked. And my feet feel like they've brushed against a fire pit.

"Ay man we shut that shit down," David manages to blurt out.

"Don't jinx us," Brian responds. "I messed up on that first step. Plus, that Kappa Nu Omega team was really good."

"Brian, have some damn confidence," Lamont jokes. "We all did great. They saved the best for last. All that's left to do, is just wait for them to finish tallying that good score, and announce us as the winner."

"Well hey look fellas," I interject. "They're strolling out there on stage, y'all trying to go back out there?" Strolling for all intent and purposes is a vertically moving line dance. My chapter loves to do this, and my brothers rarely give up the opportunity to flaunt our latest dance routines. Some may call it show boating, but I like to call it fraternity pride.

"Bet, let's go," Lamont agrees. With my informal motion seconded, we all demonstrate our vote of affirmation by running back in front of the crowd and strolling to Lil Wayne's "Lollipop."

****

We barely stroll to two songs before the music abruptly stops. The host of the show starts to command the attention of the audience, and requests all step competitors to line up according to team. It's clear to me that the judges have determined a winner, and that the host is prepared to reveal the results.

"Alright fam, time to give out this prize money," the host announces. "Can I have the sororities that competed step to the front of the stage?" As all of us Greek men move to the back, I try to predict the winner of the sororities. I'm certain that the Sigma Delta Zeta Sorority team would be victorious. That team was extremely precise with their movements, had great energy, and had an overall good theme. Who doesn't like *The Wiz*? If they lost, I would be stunned. The host calls out to the crowd, "Who do y'all think won?"

"Sigma Delta," some in the crowd yell. "Theta," others in the crowd scream. I can tell this guy is asking the question to be like every other competition host. He wants to drag out the suspense and anticipation. I usually hate when a MC does this. It is beyond aggravating. Also, I'm certain both competitors and audience members would rather know the outcome as soon as possible, so they can move on with their day, or night as is this case.

"Alright, alright, alright," the host interrupts. "Let's see who the judges are giving fifteen hundred to tonight." The venue becomes silent instantly. "And congratulations to the ladies of Sigma Delta Zeta Sorority Incorporated." The crowd swells with cheers, and countless Sigma Deltas yell their sorority call. I kind of feel bad for the other losing sororities, especially because there is no second or third place prize.

"Thank you ladies," the host continues. "Now can I have y'all fall to the back, and fellas come on up here and join me." Well, the time has finally come. Walking to the front, I unfortunately am finding the nerves that I lost while performing. I would be crushed if we lost, having spent so much time and effort practicing.

"Looks like the scores are closer in the fraternity step battle," the MC goes on to say. "There are only five points separating the top two teams. In fact, let's give it up for both these teams, the men of Kappa Nu Omega and Beta Kappa Nu." Well that's exciting. Kind of. On one hand we're in the top two, which is great. But on the other hand, five points, a simple mistake by made Brian or any one of us, could have cost us $1500.

"Alright folks, the 2008 fraternity step champion of Hamilton University is…" After hearing the MC announce the judge's decision, I feel as if I'm in a trance. I can see the crowd reacting, but I can't hear a thing. It's like I'm in a movie or something. Bringing me out of this trance is the hand I feel grab my shoulder.

"Hey, did he just say what I think he did?" Brian asks.

"Yeah I think so," I reply. "Wow!"

"How in the hell did that happen Tristan?"

April 27, 2008 (Sunday)

    For the most part, today has been quite the lazy Sunday. I intended to get up this morning and go to church, then study before I went out this evening. However, I didn't wake up until noon and haven't felt like looking in any book. Last night was very eventful. I didn't crawl into my bed until about five this morning. Following the step show, my brothers and I went to Chili's to celebrate our victory. Chili's has become my fraternity's go-to spot for celebrations. We went there last semester after my probate show, we went there last week after the new pledges' probate show, and we went there last night after we won. Last night in particular, my frat stayed at the establishment until about one in the morning. Since I don't drink, I served as the designated driver for my line brothers.

    After leaving the restaurant and bar, Willie decided to host a party of sorts in his on-campus apartment. Although I typically am not a fan of house parties, I went in an attempt to continue bonding with my brothers. Especially the new ones. The entire chapter was there with the exception of Chance. He opted to go back to his place after departing from the restaurant.

    And not only was the house party full of my brothers, but thanks to David and Randy's ability to get a word out, the party was packed wall to wall with Hamilton students. Among the student count was Mercedes. She came to the party with a few of her line sisters. It was my first time seeing her at a party, and definitely my first time seeing her a little drunk. Under the influence of alcohol, she was the smart mouthed girl I had come to know times ten.

    Not surprisingly, the on-campus security team shut down Willie's party prematurely due to noise complaints. Instead of leaving his spot and heading back to each of our own dorms or apartments, my chapter convinced me to head to IHOP. David requested that I invite Mercedes and her line sisters to join us, so I did. He and Lamont were plotting to see if they could cozy up to her sorors. By the time we left the breakfast spot, both of my line brothers walked away with a phone number. Kendrick also got a phone number. One of ladies sitting with us seemed to be quite infatuated with Kendrick in his drunken state. I remember thinking to myself, "if only she knew what I knew." Finally at about 3:45am, we all made our way back to campus to disperse for the night.

    I dropped Kendrick off last, because out of all my brothers riding with me, he lived the closest to my side of campus. Once it was just Kendrick and I left in the car, I had to ask him a question. I had to know why he got that girl's number and what he planned on doing with it.

    After I questioned him about it, he answered that he "got it to be polite." He claimed she offered it to him, and he didn't want to hurt her feelings. Kendrick was quick to let me know that he hadn't switched teams, and even joked about me being jealous. Which I promptly laughed off.

    When I got back to my apartment and finally laid down this morning, I was unable to immediately fall asleep. Mercedes decided to call my phone, and I let curiosity persuade me to answer. She said she was calling to let me know that I had better "step it up." She was referring to the fact that I hadn't been pursuing her like I should be.

    While I noticed Mercedes had been super flirtatious as of late and thought about taking her on a date, I have been dragging my feet. I'm still inexperienced in the romance department, and my lack of experience made me hesitate to pursue anything other than friendship with her and the opposite sex. However, Mercedes calling me out to "step it up" served as a catalyst for me to finally get over my apprehension. Once she accepted my invitation, we ended our conversation and I finally went to sleep.

Following such a night, it's no wonder that I woke up so late today. I'm just glad that my date with Mercedes isn't until about six this evening. I may have asked Mercedes out, but I have no idea where to take her or what to do. Thinking about the first dates I have seen play out on the small screen and in movies, it seems the standard first date entails dinner and some type of activity, usually a movie. Since this is my first date with Mercedes, and really my first date period, it's for the best that I not stray too far from the Hollywood standard. Now I just have to see what films are playing and determine where to grab a bite.

Searching the web, it seems the best option for a movie is the new Tina Fey movie, *Baby Mama*. I'm not sure if Mercedes will find the movie entertaining or not, but I've seen a few skits with Tina Fey on *Saturday Night Live*, and most of them I found funny. So I'm hoping this movie will prove to be a good choice. With the first part of the date planned, it's now time to think about where we will eat dinner.

Selecting a restaurant requires a little more thought. I want to go somewhere moderately nice, but I also want to stay within my college student budget. I don't want to take her somewhere expensive, and then be on a milk and cereal diet until payday. In addition, I want to stay away from places I don't have too much knowledge of or haven't read good reviews about.

Sifting through restaurant options in the area on my laptop, I remember Denise told me about P.F. Chang's. She raved about this place when she went with her parents a few weeks ago. I'll just take Mercedes here, and be done with it. I'm not going to let planning the date stress me out more than the actual date itself. I refuse.

****

"Hey what's up Mercedes," I ask as she climbs into my car. She looks great. Mercedes has on these navy blue pants that hug her from her ankle to the lowest part of her back. The pants even seem to make her butt look bigger. On top, she has on this bright yellow halter-top shirt, showing a peak of her navel.

"I guess we are up," she replies with a grin. "So let's go do this thing. And it better be good too!"

"Dang Mercedes! You just can't let me take you on a date without coming at me sideways, can you? Now sit back and relax! I got this." I can't help but feel gratified knowing that I successfully shut her up.

"Fine boy," she mumbles while fighting off a smile.

****

"Steele party of two," the hostess at P.F. Chang shrieks. Mercedes and I promptly follow the employee to our table. After a two-hour movie, and a thirty-minute wait to be seated, I'm definitely ready to eat.

"I guess you think you're cute or something tonight," she said with a sarcastic tone.

"Nope," I start. "I know I'm cute or something," I laugh. She giggles with me.

"Whatever Tristan! I'll admit I've had a pretty decent time so far. You've done alright. Thank you." I'm shocked by her confession. The vulnerable side of Mercedes is always nice to see. And rare.

"Well that's good, next time you take me out," I joke. Although I expect to go out with her again, I don't really anticipate that she would be paying for it. However, if she insisted, then I would oblige her.

"Oh we'll see about that," she snickers.

"By the way, did you call me Tristan?" I ask. If that's the case, this date must be going better than I thought. Up until now, I didn't realize she knew my mother had given me a real name.

"Well that's your name ain't it?" she fires back.

"Yeah it is, but...nevermind." It's probably best I not ruin a good thing by calling attention to it.

****

Now that it's the end of the date, I know we've gotten to the most important part. How Mercedes and I end this date will determine whether there will be another one in my future. No matter how well tonight has gone up until this point, it won't matter if it ends horribly. I was made aware of this fact again by TV shows and movies. To end my first date the right way, I start by parking my car in front of her dorm room.

"Alright Tristan," Mercedes begins. "All jokes aside, I enjoyed tonight." She reaches for the passenger car door handle as if to exit the vehicle.

"Well hey, you're not the worst date in the world," I kid.

"Ha, okay!" Mercedes drops her hand away from the car door handle, and she turns her body to face mine. I'm not sure if the moment has finally arrived or not, but the way she is now looking at me makes me think it's time for the all-important first kiss. I practiced for this occasion back in high school by ashamedly making out with my forearm. The moment never happened back then, but it could happen right here and now. I unbuckle my seatbelt, and turn my body toward her. However, I choose not to look her in the eyes. I'm afraid that if I do, she will be able to see the eagerness mixed with trepidation. Before I get the chance to over analyze this situation, it happens. She kisses me. The lip gloss she used to coat her soft lips makes her taste like a strawberry milkshake. And just like that, it's over.

"Oh alright," I slur. That's the least awkward thing I could think to say. Mercedes then gets out of the car. Closing the door, she looks back at me.

"Don't forget to text me later," she seductively instructs. By her saying that, I know she liked the kiss. I thought the lip-lock was nice, but I didn't feel the fireworks that people talk about. I didn't feel like I was floating on cloud nine. I just didn't feel anything.

Maybe I was so focused on the fact that this was my first kiss, that I missed the opportunity to feel the spark. In response to Mercedes' command, I simply nod as if that that's the cool thing to do. Once she enters her building, I turn on my car engine and head back to my own dorm room. Wanting to share my recent life developments, I pick up my phone and dial my ace boon Denise to fill her in.

July 12, 2008 (Saturday)

I still can't believe I'm preparing to go to a club. Alex, Isaac, and Darius decided they wanted to go out tonight, and pressured me into going with them. Although this is my first time going, my friends have been one time prior when Alex and Isaac visited Darius at college this past fall. I had an excuse not to go then because I was in the midst of trying to become a Beta. This time I have no excuse to give since we are all at home for the summer, and I'm not joining anything.

As the club novice, I'm rummaging through my closet to determine what I should wear. Looking at the venue's website to view photos, I got an idea of what's appropriate. I narrow it down to wearing a dark pair of blue jeans and some tan loafers so far, but what I can't decide on is which button up shirt to wear. I'll either wear this light blue denim one, or this red and white plaid one. Going back and forth between the two options, my phone rings.

"Hello," I answer.

"How's it going T?" Kendrick inquires on the other end of the phone.

"I'm good Ken. I'm getting ready for tonight. Do you already know what you're wearing?" I invited Kendrick to come out with me and my friends. He opted to stay in the area for the summer instead of returning home to Portsmouth, Virginia. Not only did he claim to find it boring back home and didn't want to go back for three months; but, he also registered for summer classes at Hamilton so he can graduate next spring. Since he still didn't know too many people in the area outside of Beta Kappa Nu, I thought it would be nice to invite him out.

"Yeah T, I got something figured out over here. And you?"

"I'm still working on it. I'll be there to pick you up around eleven." I'm going to go swing by Kendrick's student apartment and get him before going to D.C. He and I are going to meet up with Alex and the rest of the fellas at the club.

"Okay cool," he responds. "I was just calling to ask what time you were coming by to get me. And thanks again for the invite!"

****

For some reason this forty-five minute ride from Manassas to Alexandria to pick up Kendrick seems exceptionally long today. During this commute however, I find myself obsessing about tonight. It will be my first time partying at a club, and the first time Kendrick will be hanging out with my best friends. I can't help but think about various scenarios in which this night could become a disaster.

What if I wind up looking like a complete geek in the club? What if Kendrick gets drunk and makes things weird between us again? What if he becomes attracted to my friends? What if my friends detect Kendrick is gay, and then apply the "guilt by association" theory and think I'm gay? All these "what ifs," as unnecessary as they may be, are racing through my mind.

Arriving at Kendrick's apartment, I know I have to start thinking positively about this night. I have to think this night will consist of nothing but good times and good laughs. A night for the books.

"Sup T," Kendrick says as he opens my passenger car door.

"Hey Ken! So how do you like staying up here for the summer?"

"It's getting better," he replies. "I'm doing pretty well in my classes so far, and I just started that student internship thing with the National Institute of Mental Health. Plus, I've been recently hanging out with Bryan." I naturally assume he's referring to our fraternity brother Brian.

"Oh really," I begin. "How is our line brother doing? I haven't spoken to him in a few weeks."

"Me either! I'm actually talking about the Bryan that is in the choir with you." This development catches me a little off guard. I remember when Bryan hit on me my freshman year, and I wonder if he did the same with Kendrick. In an effort to try not to assume, I attempt to play detective.

"Is that right," I insincerely chuckle. "Bryan is cool people. I'm glad you met a new 'friend' for the summer." I put extra emphasis on the word friend. If Kendrick corrects me by insisting that the two of them are indeed just friends, then I will know nothing else is going on. This is a trick I have seen play out in a few scenarios, and it should work here too. Kendrick isn't the best of liars, so if he says there's nothing more between him and Bryan, I'll be able to tell if he's being truthful.

"Whoa, chill T! I've been on a few low key dates with him in the city, so I won't call him more than an associate just yet." His candid revelation makes me speechless. Deep down I was hoping he would say in no uncertain terms that he and Bryan were just hanging out as acquaintances. I find myself feeling some type of way. I can't quite pinpoint what I'm feeling, but I'm sure I'm not a fan of it.

"Okay, well you two have fun and what not." That's all I can muster up to say, while I'm trying to make sense of my emotions. As weird and pathetic as it may sound, I think I may be jealous. Oddly enough, I may actually be jealous that someone else has captured the attention of Kendrick. But this would be crazy, because I told him I didn't like him in that way. And I'm not gay. Heck, I should be thrilled he redirected his focus. Plus, I've technically still been trying to talk to Mercedes, even with her gone for the summer. So I really should be unbothered by Kendrick and Bryan doing their thing.

"Alrighty then T. So anyways, you ready for your big night club debut?" I can tell he is brushing off my comment and changing the topic of conversation so things don't get awkward.

"As ready as I can be," I answer. "I'm still a little anxious about going, but I told my friends I would go, so here I am. Hope we aren't at this place all night."

"Man if I didn't know any better, I would think you were sixty-five instead of twenty," Kendrick laughs. "How about this, if you get tired of being in the club, just shoot me a text and I'll make up an excuse why I need you to take me back to my apartment. Cool?"

"Alright, works for me Ken. Thanks!" I really do appreciate him being willing to do this for me. Now if I want to leave the club early, I won't look like so much of a party pooper to my friends. Kendrick is willing to provide me with a legit alibi.

"No problem grandpa." I simply scoff at his name-calling.

****

"I.D.," demands the Hulk-like bouncer working the door at Paradise. Paradise is the new eighteen and up club in D.C. Kendrick already walked through the entrance, and I'm about to do the same once the bouncer returns my driver's license.

"Alright sir, have a good night." With the bouncer's words, I take my I.D. and walk into the venue. As Kendrick and I prepare to do a search of the place for my friends, I hear someone holler out my name.

"Tristan! Ay, yo Tristan!" Turning to locate the source of the voice, I see Alex standing over by the bar. Behind him are Isaac and Darius. It's funny to see them by the bar, considering they all have a big "x" drawn on the back of their hand like me. None of us are old enough to drink, with the exception of Kendrick.

"Lex, what's up?" I begin. "How long y'all been here?"

"We got here about ten minutes ago," he responds. "You ready?"

"Yeah T-man," Darius interrupts. "Are you ready, because it's time to go bag these females. Bet I get the most numbers."

"Naw that will be me," Isaac protests.

"Well before y'all start this competition, this is Kendrick," I said as I point to him towering behind me.

"Cool, I'm Isaac," Isaac states as he leads the dapping up of my frat brother. One by one, my friends greet him with a hand embrace.

"So Kendrick, you think you're gonna bag more numbers than your boy Tristan?" Darius chimes in.

"Bruh, you know T-man is talking to that girl he works with," Alex interjects. "He prolly can't compete."

"Whoa calm down," I chuckle. "I told y'all that Mercedes and I went on a few dates, but we're not in an official relationship yet. In fact, since she went home for the summer, we decided that she can do her and I can do me. But we still talk." Mercedes and I thought it would be best not to start something as serious as a relationship, since she would be gone for the duration of the three month long school break. We agreed to revisit the idea when she comes back in August. So for now, I guess we are in limbo.

"Whatever that means," Alex mumbles looking confused.

"Yeah in that case, you definitely better get some digits my dude," Darius instructs. "Let the games begin."

****

It's been about an hour and a half into my experience at Paradise, and I'm ready to go. Even though I've enjoyed the music and hanging out with my friends, I'm annoyed by how hot it is in here. I even think about moving, and the sweat beads start rolling down my forehead. And the number of drunken people stepping on my shoes and bumping into me is beyond irritating. It's like no one has ever heard of the term "excuse me." So I sent Kendrick a text, and told him I'm ready. I'm just waiting for his reply, or for the announcement of his excuse for needing to leave.

In terms of this numbers game we are playing, the last time I checked, the person leading the competition is ironically Kendrick. He may be gay, but he has a way with the opposite sex that is unmatched by the rest of us. Plus, I think he benefits greatly from the fact that he is tall, muscular, and rather handsome. I on the other hand, am in last place. I didn't try that hard to get numbers. I just didn't feel like playing.

As I see Kendrick finally emerge from the sea of girls vying for his attention, my phone starts to vibrate in my pocket. Looking at my phone, I see Kendrick's message confirming he is ready to implement the exit strategy. This confirmation puts the biggest smile I've had on my face all night. Knowing that I'm about to leave, I scan the club to locate Alex, Isaac, and Darius to tell them goodbye. I find them grinding on some girls in a line against the wall. Once Kendrick walks up beside me, we head over to my friends. In an effort not to fully interrupt their dances, I simply tell them I have to take Kendrick home, and I'll see them later. They don't seem to care too much at the moment since they are having a *good* time. I guess I really didn't need much of a reason to leave after all.

"Hey Ken," I say to him as we make it outside of the club. "How are you so smooth with women? I thought you were..? Well you know."

"If you mean gay, then yes I am," He quips. "And just because I'm gay doesn't negate the fact that girls find me attractive and charming. And if you're wondering whether I lied to these girls that gave me their number, the answer is no. Had they asked about my sexuality, I would have gladly shared. The question you should be asking is why you let a gay man show you and your friends up tonight in this so-called numbers game?" Kendrick is so smug right now.

"Point taken Ken!"

"Good T! I'm gonna have to school you on how to talk to females." We both chuckle and continue walking to my car.

Junior Year

Chapter 5: Fall 2008

September 19, 2008 (Friday)

"About damn time I get to see my brother from another," Denise jokes. "We haven't been out to eat and chill since the semester started about four weeks ago. Bet you've had time for Mercedes and those Betas." Although she's joking, I can tell she feels a little disappointed about not meeting up as frequently as we did in prior semesters. Beta Kappa Nu has been taking up a lot of my time since I pledged, and when Mercedes returned this semester we picked up dating again. In addition, I still retain a leadership position with the choir and am still a member of BSAS. I chose not to take an executive board position this year with the latter. I didn't think I could adequately designate the time and commitment it takes. All in all though, I've been keeping quite busy, but slacking in my best friend duties.

"Dang Denise, I apologized earlier. The beginning of this semester has just been a little crazy. And heck, I let you pick the movie and restaurant for tonight."

"Mmhmm Tristan."

"Denise will you close my car door so we can make it to the movie before it starts. You know I hate missing the previews."

"Okay, okay," she scoffs while closing my car door. "So what's going on with you and Mercedes? Y'all together or not?" I had tried to explain the answer to this question to

Denise before, but that was somewhat hard to do. The thing between Mercedes and I is complicated. I like her, and I can tell she likes me, but both of us seem hesitant to commit to one another. Even with her back from her summer away at home. I have never been in a relationship before, and the last relationship Mercedes was in ended terribly. It's like the both of us let our commitment issues keep us stuck in neutral so to speak.

"Like I said, we are just dating and taking things slow," I reply. "Not rushing to get in anything."

"Hmm, if you say so Tristan. But I'll tell you now, if she is toying with you or hurts your heart, I will drag her sorority ass in these streets." I loudly bust out laughing at Denise's protective nature.

"You know you couldn't do that," I snicker. "In other news, what's going on with your love life?" I don't know if this has become a sore subject for her or not, but I ask anyway.

"Truth be told, I did some thinking over the summer, and I've made a decision," Denise tells me. "I'm going to be a woman of today, and ask a guy out." I'm shocked to the point my jaw drops. Denise is the closest thing I know to a modern southern belle, so for her to ask a guy out is huge. I pick up my jaw to make an inquiry.

"Well, who is this mystery man that you plan on asking out? Or do you not have one in mind?"

"I do have a man in mind," she begins to answer. "It's this real fine chocolate brotha on campus. He's a senior with a great body, great personality, and great potential to be successful."

"Sounds like a decent enough guy," I gasp. "You better scoop him up before some other girl does. Do I know this dude?"

"Actually you do know him Tristan. I'm going to ask Kendrick out." I really hope I heard her wrong, or that she said Kendrick by mistake.

"Say what now," I probe.

"Kendrick! You know your frat brother? I'm going to ask him if he wants to go out with me." With the confirmation of the name, I find myself frantically trying to determine what I should say. Denise is like a sister to me. How can I not warn her that the guy she likes is gay? However, how can I blurt out a secret of Kendrick's that not mine to tell? We have a brotherly bond, and although he isn't embarrassed about who he is, I know he prefers to keep his private life private. In order to protect both relationships, I must say what I can to sway Denise from pursuing my line brother without divulging his sexuality.

"You don't think it's weird trying to date your friend?" I'm hopeful that playing up this friend angle would discourage her.

"I know he is our friend and your brother, but I honestly like him." Sensing her determination with asking him out, I've got to try another approach.

"Okay I hear ya," I state. "I still think you may want to redirect your focus on another guy, because I believe Kendrick may be dating someone." I knew that he'd been loosely involved with Bryan from the choir over the summer, so I play the "he's unavailable" card with Denise. I'm crossing my fingers that she won't ask any follow-up questions.

"Oh wow he's with someone? Is it with a girl that I know?" Figures she would ask follow-up questions.

"Yeah he is. And it's no girl that you know." Which is definitely not a lie. As far as I know, Bryan has all of his man bits.

"Well damn! I guess I do have to find another man. If you hear about him being single again, let me know." Clearly for the purpose of protecting everyone's interest, Kendrick will always be taken as far as she is concerned. "Onto the next one in the meantime!"

"Exactly," I second. "Find you an available boo.

October 3, 2008 (Friday)

"Ay Tristan, you sure you're not trying to drink," David asks. All my brothers and I are in David's student apartment getting ready to head to the campus party being thrown by Kappa Nu Omega. While they are pre-gaming with a party punch Willie and Randy made, I'm sitting here drinking a bottle of water waiting until it's time to leave.

"Naw David I'm good," I answer. "I'm still not drinking man." I am still quite the anomaly amongst frat men and college students since I choose not to drink alcohol. However as of late, I've been increasingly more interested in at least trying it. So, saying no to an offer of alcohol is becoming harder and harder.

"Tristan you should taste the punch," David insists. "Just sampling it won't get you drunk." People who know me know that the main reason I don't drink is because the Bible cautions against getting drunk. And then there's the fact, I'm not even twenty-one yet.

"Hey David, ease up on Tristan," Kendrick interjects. "You know he's not into that kind of stuff." Even though I appreciate Kendrick trying to defend me, I'm grown and quite capable of speaking for myself.

"Chill Ken, it's okay," I tell him. "You know what David, pour me some!" Suddenly, the room grows quiet. Everyone is obviously stunned by my request.

"Whoa really?" David questions sounding shocked. "Well let's get you a cup!" I don't know if I've ever heard him sound so eager.

"Are you sure about this?" Kendrick whispers to me while grabbing my shoulder.

"Yeah Ken, I'm sure," I reply. "Now you relax and worry about yourself."

"Here you go," David states as he gave me my red Solo Cup. I have been around enough college students to know that a red Solo Cup is the unofficial cup for an alcoholic beverage. As I raise the cup to sniff the contents, my brothers' eyes are unshakably glued on me. I guess this is a momentous occasion for not only me, but for everyone. Without any further delay, I put the rim up to my lips and take a sip. That sip causes my Beta brothers to yell in excitement.

"Haha, Tristan welcome to the club," Randy exclaims.

"Yeah buddy, I'll drink to that," Willie hollers. We all laugh and join him in taking a gulp.

"This punch is pretty good," I admit. "I'm almost done with this David. Pour me some more."

"Alright bruh," he responds. "Anybody else need to be topped off?" Nearly everyone requests a refill, except Kendrick. "Kendrick, you don't want anymore?"

"Nope, I'm good," he answers. "It's T's first time drinking, and someone has to make sure he doesn't get into trouble."

"Alright Papa Bear," David jokes. "But for real, good looking out."

"Guys, I'm not getting drunk," I insist. I want to remind them that I'm still here, and can hear them. "Besides this punch is like juice, I'll be fine."

"This is definitely more than juice," David counters. "Trust me on that."

"If you say so," I mumble under my breath.

****

"Man T, you've been strolling at this party all night," Kendrick notes. "Are you okay?"

"Yeah I'm just hot," I reply. "Is it time to go yet?" After all the dancing and strolling I've been doing tonight, I find myself sweaty and exhausted. And while I'm not sick to my stomach, slurring my words, seeing double, or experiencing any of the other symptoms of drunkenness, I'm feeling differently than usual. It's like I'm freer.

"Well the party is not supposed to end for another hour," Kendrick tells me. I can tell even in my influenced state, that he is getting a kick out of my alcohol induced high. "If you are ready to go though, I'll walk you back to your place."

"You know what, let's get out of here Ken." I want to tell the rest of my frat brothers bye, but my pressing desire to leave trumps my desire to be polite.

"Alright T, let's bounce!" Leaving, I can see half of my brothers dripping in sweat behind some of this year's latest bunch of freshman girls. The other brothers are still strolling around the room. Once outside the party, I'm soothed by the rush of cool air from the October night.

"Ken, I can't believe I drank liquor tonight. I kind of feel bad, but at the same time I feel so good."

"Can't lie, I'm shocked my damn self! But I kind of like this Tristan. You seem much more relaxed."

"Thanks I think..." Kendrick makes it seem like I'm uptight sober.

"T, don't get offended or anything. You have to admit, you're usually so guarded. Most of the time you're so concerned by what people think of you, that you don't allow yourself to be the true you. I'm not saying you're fake, but I'm saying you rarely let the world see the many dimensions of Tristan Steele."

"Way to clean that up," I smirk. I'm kind of fascinated by his take on me. He is right, and I know it. "I'll see if I can work on that. But hey, are you hungry?"

"I could eat, you want me to drive us to IHOP or something?" he proposes. Although pancakes drenched in butter pecan syrup sound good, I'm not quite in the mood to sit down in a restaurant.

"Actually, I was gonna say I'm cooking breakfast when I get back to my apartment, and did you want some?"

"Uh T, are you even okay to be cooking? And aren't you afraid of waking up Carter?"

"Don't worry Ken, I'm good to cook. And I can't wake up Carter tonight, because he is gone until Sunday visiting some friends from high school. So do you want some food or not?"

"Alright sure, thanks," he chuckles. He's probably chuckling because he doubts me and my ability to cook breakfast, which is making me determined to get back to my apartment and cook a breakfast better than most people's big mama.

****

"While I get breakfast ready, do you want something to drink?" I ask Kendrick as we walk through the threshold of my on-campus apartment.

"Sure T, I'll just have some water," he answers. I bend over to grab him a bottle out of the fridge, and grab one for myself as well. In getting back up, I feel the sudden need to sit down. Between the alcohol and all the strolling, I guess my body needs to sit down and rest for a minute or two.

"Here you go," I mumble to Ken as I give him his water and sit on the couch next to him.

"What happened to this grand breakfast you're supposed to be cooking?" he sarcastically inquires with a grin on his face.

"Just give me a minute Ken, I'll get breakfast ready. On another note, I want to say how glad I am we got over that little bump in our friendship. You're a great person to have around." I'm not sure why I feel the urge to rehash the past, or make this confession.

"Ha, I'm glad we got over that bump too. Sorry again for making you so uncomfortable T."

"No, again I'm sorry for blowing up at you," I reiterate. "And you didn't make me feel uncomfortable necessarily. I was actually flattered. At the time when you were telling me how you felt, I wasn't prepared to receive that."

"Oh, okay," he responds. I can tell he is trying to process what I'm saying. "Well let's just let the past be the past."

"I agree, but I feel like this conversation has needed to happen for quite some time now." At this point, my mouth is taking me deeper into a conversation my brain is still too unnerved to have. But, this liquid courage is giving me a boost of sorts.

"Um okay…I'm listening T."

"Ken, let's go back to that night I came over to your place and we nursed each other wounds. In the midst of all the

Vaseline rubbing, I noticed you got aroused. Also, I noticed that night that I got... got... well I got aroused too." Here we go, I'm finally about to be completely honest with Kendrick. And really myself.

"Okay, now let me stop you and ask you this," Kendrick interrupts. "I know why I was hard, but why were you?" This is a question I asked myself several times. Each time I found myself in denial, and blamed my erection on any and everything but the truth. Despite me feeling freer and wanting to be more candid with him, I'm doubting now if I can fully commit.

"Not sure what was up with me," I mutter.

"Tristan, if you're not ready or capable of having this discussion honestly, then why don't we just leave it in the past and move on." He is clearly getting a little agitated by me giving this cop out answer. I don't like seeing his frustration, and know he deserves better.

"Don't get upset," I say while standing up. If I'm going to try to utter the absolute truth, I don't want to be sitting down right next to him.

"Sorry, but what should my reaction be then?" he counters. "Look, I think I'll pass on breakfast. You should probably just get some rest. I'll talk to you later." He gets up and moves toward the front door. Before he could walk by me, I reach out and grab his arm.

"Kendrick, I think I like you too." The words just rush out of my mouth in a faint whisper.

"Wait, what did you say? You think you like me?"

"Yeah, I think I like you," I confirm. I've just opened an industrial size can of worms that I'm not sure can be closed.

"You think you like me? T, what does that mean?" I don't understand why he is making this more complicated for me. How many times does he need me to say it?

"Ken, it means I like you. And not like I like my friends from back home. I like you in the way I'm supposed to like a girl. In the way I should truly like Mercedes. I know when you came clean to me months ago and told me how you felt, I denied the connection you said you sensed between us. But I wasn't ready then to admit I sense it too. Heck, I'm really not sure I'm ready now, but I think it's time you knew." By now, Kendrick's body language and facial expression have changed. He went from being pissed and ready to leave, to now appearing intrigued and ready to hear more.

"Really," he questions. "Why did you feel you couldn't tell me this back then?"

"I shouldn't be having these kinds of feelings for a guy," I go on to say. "It goes against everything I was raised to believe. It goes against the Christian principles I was taught all my life. I couldn't admit that I'm attracted to you, and that I want you. So for months, I've tried to suppress my feelings. That's the main reason why I've been trying so hard to make things work with Mercedes. Don't get me wrong, she is a great person. But I know in my heart of hearts that doesn't matter because she is not you."

I'm becoming overwhelmed with emotions, and my eyes are filling up with tears. All I can do to stop from full out crying is turn away from Kendrick, and roll my eyes to the top of my head. Not only am I regretting this conversation I initiated, but I'm also regretting the drinks I had earlier that led me to it.

"Wow T," Kendrick says as he grabs my arm and pulls me in for an embrace. Being comforted in his arms feels so good. My head is pressed against his chest, and the smell of

Calvin Klein cologne from his shirt is flirting with my nostrils. Nestled between his firm pecs, I take a deep breath and allow myself to be consoled. "Tristan it's alright, I understand. Believe me, I do."

"You do?" I ask as I pull my head of his body and take a step back.

"Yeah I do," he repeats while intently looking at me. I love the fact that he seems to be sympathetic to my dilemma. Having expressed all of my feelings and then having them validated and understood by Kendrick, I find myself attracted to him even more. I mean my hormones are pulsating. I badly want to disregard my apprehension, and outwardly express the feelings I've kept bottled up inside for nearly a year.

"Ken," I utter. I then grab his beautifully flawless face, and bring it down in front of mine. Before I have time to convince myself not to do it, I kiss him. It's not an elaborate kiss, but a simple one right on his lips in the middle of my living room. My closed lips are pressed firmly against his. The soft pillows that serve as the gateway to his mouth taste like the sweetest dessert I've ever had.

"Whoa Tristan," Kendrick gasps as he pulls away from me. "Are you sure you want to be doing this? What about everything you just said?"

"I know all the stuff I said, but… well I want you."

"Okay T." Kendrick pulls me back into him and begins kissing me again. This time there is nothing simple about it. Our lips are no longer closed, and our mouths are vastly intertwined. This kiss is full of the passion that I've always imagined a kiss should be. I'm not certain how long we've been in this lip lock, but I pull away from him only to grab his right hand. I start leading him to my bedroom. I haven't the slightest clue as to what I'm leading Kendrick to do, but it feels right.

Upon entering my room, we inch closer to my bed and I start taking off my shirt. While I'm disrobing, he is doing the same. It's clear he wants me as bad as I want him. In the blink of an eye, we both find ourselves standing in front of each other in our purest form, and ready. I can't help but survey his tall chocolate body. His nude chest perfectly chiseled, and shoulders ripped as if he carries the weight of the world. His abs are so carefully carved, creating a picturesque six pack. If he ever tells me he moonlights as a superhero, I'll believe him based on his physique alone. As my eyes continue to move down his body, I become captivated by his manhood. Although I had got a glimpse of it before, I didn't have the view of it like I have now. The only thing distracting me from its wondrous length and breathtaking thickness, are the number of bulging veins.

"You alright?" Kendrick whispers with a deep masculine sensuality.

"Yeah Ken, I'm good. Just looking at how sexy your body is." Any reservations I had about pursuing my true feelings were checked at my bedroom door. I'm ready to succumb to my *natural* desires.

"Thanks T. You know I think you're the finest man at Hamilton. I've thought that since I first transferred here." The fact that he is so into me is causing me to tap into an inner primal instinct that has been buried underneath my virginity. I throw Kendrick on my bed flat on his back. While most of his body lie horizontally across my comforter, his above average junior is vertically standing at attention. I might be a novice at this type of activity, but somehow I know exactly what to do.

"Oh damn, Tristan baby!" His exclamation paired with his pulsating captain lets me know that he's enjoying our sexual voyage.

October 4, 2008 (Saturday)

"Good morning," Kendrick says as I open my eyes. He's lying right next to me in my extra-long twin size bed, with his feet dangling off the end of it.

"Morning Ken," I reply. With a clear mind, one free of alcoholic influence and sexual desires, I realize the magnitude of all that was said and done last night. There are so many questions rattling through my mind. For example, am I still a virgin? After all, no penetration occurred. And how I could allow myself to wind up in this position? More importantly, now that I am in this position with Kendrick, does that mean I'm officially gay? Then there is kicker. What does God now think of me?

"You okay?" I can only assume Kendrick is asking me this because I have a worried expression on my face.

"Yeah I guess, just thinking," I respond.

"Did I do something wrong T? Is this about last night?"

"No, you did nothing wrong," I tell him. "And last night was more than I imagined it would be." I didn't lie to Kendrick, because he did nothing I didn't want, and in the moment of last night, I was extremely pleased.

"Then what is it? I know something is up with you."

"Nothing I'm fine," I counter. "Hey what time does it say on my alarm clock?" As he rolls over to check the time, I search my brain for an excuse as to why I have to get up and why he has to leave. I need to get out of this room and away from him so I can think.

"It's 11:10," he says.

"Oh crap, I'm supposed to pick up Denise in twenty minutes," I rattle off. "Told her I would take her to the mall." While I did promise to take Denise to the mall, we aren't scheduled to leave until 2:30.

"Ah for real?" he questions. "I was hoping we could really talk about what went down last night, and how we go forward from here." We probably do need to discuss these things, but I can't talk about them now.

"I hear you Ken. Can I call you later?"

"Sure T." He looks a little disappointed. "Hit me up when you finish." He then gets up and searches for his clothes on my bedroom floor. I feel bad for doing this to him, but for the sake of my sanity, he's got to go ASAP.

"Thanks for understanding," I mutter.

"No problem," he sighs. Once fully clothed, he begins exiting my room.

"Wait Ken," I call out. "If you wouldn't mind, can we keep what happened last night between us?"

"Um yeah man," Kendrick scoffs. "Have fun!" Only after hearing the front door of my apartment open and shut, did I myself get out of bed.

Now up, I bolt to my bathroom to take a shower. I want to jump in steaming hot water and lather myself in soap. I plan to scrub every remnant of last night off my body. That includes bodily fluids, as well as the shame. Words can't describe the amount of guilt I'm experiencing at this very moment. I feel I let God down by giving into temptation. Like I failed a test in my Christian walk.

While cleaning off in the shower, I keep having flashbacks of me and Kendrick. Each memory that my mind rehashes makes me feel worse. And I can only hope Kendrick will keep what happened between us, between us. The last thing I need to deal with is others' judgments. My God! What did I do?

October 11, 2008 (Saturday)

    It's been a week since I awakened in Kendrick's arms. Although I told him I would call him back after my mall trip with Denise last week, I failed to do so. I just didn't know what to say to him, and still don't. While I don't want to make him feel as if I lured him into my bedroom to satisfy my own sexual curiosity, I also don't want to lead him on to believe we could be something more than friends right now, or perhaps ever. Not sure what to say to Kendrick, I've said nothing.

    To avoid Kendrick and a potentially awkward conversation, I became a hermit crab for the week. I went to class and work only. Because I live in a student apartment, I've been cooking my meals these past few days so I didn't have to venture out to campus dining. In addition, I explained to all the organizations I'm involved with that I wouldn't be able to make it to any meetings or events for the time being. I made sure to skip all Beta Kappa Nu events especially. Thankfully, my plan of avoidance has been working so far.

    Perhaps the only problem I found with my plan, is the fact that it caused my phone to explode with calls and texts from people inquiring about my whereabouts. Denise reached out to me wondering why I cancelled our dinner plans we had scheduled for Wednesday night. I just told her I haven't been feeling that well.

    I also had to deal with Mercedes' inquiries as to why I fell off the grid. Since she stopped working for the Office of Admissions, I didn't necessarily have to see her every day unless we planned to meet up; although, we usually got together for lunch or dinner a few times throughout the week. However, this week I didn't extend an offer to her for anything, and I declined all of her invitations. I'm sure her feelings are hurt about the way I've been dodging her, but what am I to do? Even though we aren't officially in a relationship and just dating, I somehow feel as if I cheated on her. I couldn't bear to look at her, knowing I had been with someone else. Let alone a man. Seeing her face to face, would make me feel like a real life manifestation of the infamous DL man. So I also told her I've been sick too.

While continuing to sit in the loudness of my thoughts, I'm interrupted by a knock on my apartment front door. I can't imagine who is knocking on my door before noon on a Saturday. Unfortunately, I can't rely on Carter to answer the door because I heard him and his girlfriend leave the apartment about an hour ago. Getting out of my bed and looking for clothes to throw on to answer the door, I again hear another knock.

"Just a second," I yell out, hoping the person would hear me and wait. I throw on some sweatpants and a t-shirt I find in my hamper, and hurry to answer the door. Something is telling me to look through the peep hole first, but I ignore my instinct. Opening the door, I try to hide my utter shock.

"Oh so you still exist," Kendrick snipes with a stern tone and serious expression to match. I can tell he is upset, because when he gets angry his jaw visibly tightens and a vein runs across the right side of his forehead just above his eyebrow.

"Hey Ken," I softly reply, as if I'm a kid that just got busted by his parents. "Come on in." He walks through the doorway and sits down on the couch in the very spot he sat the last time he was here.

"I mean damn Tristan, what's up with you? It's been a week since I woke up in your bed, and I have to hunt you down to talk about it? You haven't called or sent a text, and you won't respond when I contact you. To top it off, you've been pretty much M.I.A. on campus. I'm not an idiot. I know you've been avoiding me. The question I have is why?" In the minute Kendrick has been here, he has managed to make me feel even lower than I did before his arrival.

"I'm sorry for avoiding you, but it's complicated," I tell him.

"Complicated? Tristan, what the hell is complicated about just talking to me?"

"Ken, I don't know how to explain it."

"I suggest you find a way," he demands. "You owe me an explanation as to why you led me to believe you wanted me and led me into your bedroom; then, turned around and did everything you could to duck and dodge me for the past several days. Do I need to get you some alcohol again so you can open up?" I understand his frustration, but the alcohol comment is a low blow. Instead of getting pissed about it, I decide to let what he said roll off my back.

"It's hard for me to describe how I'm feeling, because I don't know myself," I blurt out. "I have this undeniable connection with you that I've yet to feel with anyone. And last week when we spent the night together it felt so good and right. But I've betrayed my relationship with God by what we did. That's hard for me to deal with. Not knowing how to balance these two perspectives and how to move forward with you, I've stayed away." Trying to read his face after what I just told him is a bit difficult. He relaxes his jaw and the vein above his eyebrow disappears, so I know he's not angry anymore. But, he looks concerned and confused.

"Well…um," Kendrick mumbles.

"Wait a second let me finish," I interrupt. "I've not only avoided you, but I've avoided everyone as much as possible. I needed time to make sense of everything and figure out what being with you means for me and my self-identity.

All week long, I've been praying and reading the Bible in search for answers."

"Did you find any?" he questions.

"I can't say for certain that I have," I reply. "What I can say is that I've read a few verses of the Bible, and they've validated the convicted spirit I have. The verses confirm to me that what happened that night shouldn't have happened, and can't happen again. But at the same time, a part of my heart really wants to explore something more with you because I do like you." I wonder if he understands where I'm coming from, because he is simply nodding his head.

"I see," he calmly states. "Can I ask what verses you read?"

"I read a few verses like I said. I know I read Leviticus 20:13." Suddenly the text came to my mind as if it's etched in my brain. "It read 'If a man lies with a man as one lies with a woman, both of them have done what is detestable. They must be put to death; their blood will be on their own heads'" Kendrick just keeps nodding and grinning. I have no idea what he finds humorous in this situation.

"Okay T, what other verses did you read?"

"Well I also looked at Romans 1:18-32. Specifically at verses 26 to 28." I don't know word for word what theses verses state, so I go to my room to grab my Bible. "Hold on one second."

"No problem," he responds.

Walking back into the living room, I quickly search for the passage. "Here we go Ken. '[26] Because of this, God gave them over to shameful lusts. Even their women exchanged natural relations for unnatural ones. [27] In the same way the men also abandoned natural relations with women and were inflamed with lust for one another. Men committed indecent acts with other men, and received in themselves the due penalty for their perversion. [28] Furthermore, since they did not think it worthwhile to retain the knowledge of God, he gave them over to a depraved mind, to do what ought not to be done.'"

"These passages have really made me feel lower that low," I continue.

"I can see how reading them would make you feel that way," he replies. "Are there any other verses that you read?"

"Actually, there is another verse that comes to mind," I answer.

"Let me guess," Kendrick interjects. "You're referring to 1 Corinthians 6: 9-10?" He guesses right.

"Um yeah, how did you know?" I ask.

"T, I understand what you are going through. I understand because I've been exactly where you are. Trying to find yourself, while trying to stay true to God and Christianity."

"Wow, really Ken? You get it?" I'm thrilled to hear that someone could relate to my plight. It's ironic that the one person that I can talk to and can relate to what I'm going through, is the same person I've been ducking and dodging all week.

"Of course I get it," he confirms. "However, I wonder if you've read other parts of the Bible this week?"

"Other parts like what?" I inquire. "If you mean have I read other verses that condemn being gay, then the answer is yes."

"That's not quite what I mean T. I'm trying to ask you if you've read parts of the Bible this week that talk about God's love for his children. Take for example John 3:16 and 18." Now I know John 3:16 by heart. It's a verse that was drilled in every child's head in Sunday school. I don't know the latter verse as well, but I'm positive I've read it.

"I've read those verses before," I tell him. "Did they help you through this process?"

"Actually they did. You have your Bible there T, look over them again." Per Kendrick's instruction, I thumb through my Bible until I get to John. Once I find the 16th verse, I start to read it to myself. "'16 For God so loved the world that he gave his one and only Son, that whoever believes in him shall not perish but have eternal life.'" It reads just how I remember it.

I then proceed to read verse eighteen. "'18 Whoever believes in him is not condemned, but whoever does not believe stands condemned already because he has not believed in the name of God's one and only Son.'" Having read these two passages again, I wonder if I love God and believe in who Jesus is, would I really be condemned to an eternity in Hell for being gay.

"Well T, what do you think?"

"To be honest, they make me feel a little better about swinging this way; but, they also make me feel even more spiritually confused."

"That's to be expected," he claims. "This whole thing is new for you. When I get back to my apartment, I'll email you some more verses. And look, don't think I'm trying to sway you into being gay, especially for my own benefit. I'm just trying to offer you some more insight and perspective, so you can figure out who you are. Although I don't believe that gay and Christian are contradictory terms, that's a conclusion you will have to reach on your own with God." I appreciate Kendrick for his words of wisdom, and for not attempting to pressure me into something.

"Thanks for talking with me Ken. And I apologize again for avoiding you. Like I said, I was just trying to figure this all out. But, I could have at least communicated that to you."

"Don't worry about it," he smiles. "Now that you've explained yourself, I get it. Thank you for doing that by the way. I was starting to think you were a hit it and quit it type of dude." We both start laughing. I haven't laughed in several days, which is unusual for me. "Seriously though, my bad for letting things get that far last weekend. You really weren't ready."

"Man don't apologize for that," I insist. "We were two consenting adults."

"True," he agrees. And with that, he gets up and prepares to leave.

"Again, I can't tell you how much I appreciate you for coming over here," I say.

"You're welcome T. You know when something doesn't smell right, I'll go knocking on doors to get to the bottom of it. If you need to talk about this again, you have my number. By the way, can you do me a favor?"

"What's that?" I question.

"Don't coup yourself up in this apartment. Go back to being Super Undergrad. And as far as *us* is concerned, we are still good as brothers and friends. Anything more right now is unfair to both you and me."

"Okay bet," I confirm. "By the way, I have one more question for you. Are you going to tell Bryan what happened?"

"Why would I tell him?" he asks. "Bryan and I stopped trying to date shortly after I told you about him this past summer. The chemistry just wasn't there. But we are still friendly."

"Cool, cool," I mumble.

"What about you and Mercedes," Kendrick probes.

"Mercedes and I have never been official per say. It's complicated, but just know I was and am technically single."

"Hmm okay," he responds. "Alright, I'm getting out of here. I guess I'll talk to you later."

"Take care Ken." He then exits my apartment, and I'm again left alone with my thoughts.

November 2, 2008 (Sunday)

Roughly a month has gone by since I started going through my sexual identity crisis, and I'm no closer to figuring this all out. After talking to Kendrick that day he came by my place demanding answers, I hoped things would get better. Better as in I would no longer feel this sense of guilt. Better as in I would finally come to a determination as to my sexual orientation. Better as in I would know for certain if it is okay to move forward with Kendrick or not. Unfortunately, I'm more confused than ever, and battling what I suspect is serious depression.

Also, over the past few weeks I have begun pondering the earthly ramifications of being homosexual. Should I identify as gay, I know my mom would be crushed. I'm her only child, and I don't think she could handle her only baby being gay. While my mom has a liberal view on many topics, I don't think this topic is one of them. She and I have a great relationship, and I'd rather not put a strain on it.

Then there are my friends. More specifically my friends from back home. We all basically grew up together. They are like blood brothers to me. I know how they will respond if I tell them I like men. Alex, Isaac, and Darius tell jokes from time to time that could be considered offensive to the gay community. These jokes, combined with their excessive use of "no homo," plus their obvious discomfort around gays and lesbians, leaves me to assume being gay would lead to the ultimate destruction of our friendship. A bond that seemed life long, suddenly looks like it could have an expiration date. If friends I've had for over twelve years would disown me because of my sexuality, I imagine my Greek brotherhood would do the same. Well, my Greek brotherhood minus Kendrick.

I've also thought about my friend/sister Denise. I'm not necessarily that worried if Denise were to find out I prefer men. Out of all the people close to me, I think she perhaps would be the most supportive in this regard. However, I don't think she would take the news well that I hooked up with Kendrick. Kendrick is the one guy on campus that she expressed a genuine interest in, and I like him. Heck, I had him. I'm a little scared I crossed a line that is beyond forgiveness. The more I contemplate being gay, the more I realize that living out loud will lead to a lonely place in life.

Imagining the worst about the possibility of a homosexual future, I've desperately been attempting to "pray the gay away." I prayed numerous times that God would deliver me from my *perversion*, and that he would mold me into the good straight Christian guy I desire to be. Unfortunately, even with my prayers I still find myself in this place where I know deep down, I'm gay. Being honest with myself for the first time, I think I've known since I hit puberty. However, I was able to suppress my alternative nature up until that night with Kendrick. Now that this side of me has been released, I don't know if I can again pretend it doesn't exist.

With all the aforementioned weighing heavy on my mind, I'm lying here in my bed frustrated. I feel like I'm at a crossroads in my life, where I have to make an almost impossible decision. Either I pretend to be something I'm not, and embark on a future of unhappiness masked by fake smiles. Or, I embrace my truth, which could leave me alone and outside the will of God. I really want to find a third option, because the two I have seem unimaginable.

Racking my brain for a third option, I allow myself to consider doing something I've never thought was feasible prior to this moment. It's something that many people have chosen to do when life became too much for them to handle. Perhaps I could do like these individuals, and leave this world early by my own hands. By taking this route, I wouldn't have to worry about being unhappy, or who in my life would accept me, or God not approving of my lifestyle. I could just avoid it all, and hope I make it to see Jesus a little earlier than I originally anticipated.

If I'm really going to kill myself, that means I have to write a suicide note. I have to say a final goodbye of some sort. The only thing is, I've heard of a suicide note, but I've never read one to know how to write one. And it's not like there are "how to" books on this stuff. Thinking of ideas for my parting words, I grab my laptop to create a rough draft.

Dear Family and Friends,

I'm not quite sure where to start. I guess I'll start with the obvious. If you're reading this letter, you know by now I'm no longer with you. I wish I could give you a full explanation of why I did what I did, but unfortunately I just can't. What I will share is this, over the past several weeks, I have been dealing with this internal struggle. It's like I've been watching this fight between who I am and who I want to be go on; and, neither side wants to give up. Because of that, I've been suffering. The consequences of letting either side actually win this fight, would leave me to be the ultimate loser. I would either disappoint and lose each of you and God during my time here on earth, or I would disappoint myself and lead a life of pretending. Both possibilities are inconceivable to me. So I chose to spare myself the pain.

I know you all will probably rack your brains trying to figure out if you could have done something to prevent me from taking my life, but trust me you couldn't have. No one could have convinced me that this misery would go away. That somehow this feeling of suffocation would disappear. I've been praying for God to help me with my problem, but I can't say that I've been provided with the answers and relief that I desperately have been seeking. That's why I've opted to leave this world in hopes of making an early entrance into Heaven. At least there, I know I no longer have to deal with my earthly human struggles. At least there I will finally have peace.

Mom, I'm so sorry for the pain I've caused you.

Writing this last sentence to my mother serves as a badly needed wake up call. Thinking about the number of tears my mom would cry if her only child voluntarily left this life before her is gut-wrenching. My other relatives and friends would also be left to grieve knowing they never got to give me a proper goodbye. And I may not know if God approves of me being gay or not, but I'm pretty sure He has an issue with me trying to do his job. My time to die will come, and it's not for me to determine when that is.

There is a certain level of selfishness committing suicide. I would be selfish to leave behind such a tainted legacy. I don't want the last visual people have of me being one where I'm lying in a pool of blood, or dangling from the ceiling. It's becoming clear that suicide cannot be my option three. Although it's alluring as a quick fix and escape, it's a permanent solution to a temporary problem; and, it causes nothing but heartache for loved ones left to deal with the aftermath.

Tired of thinking and realizing that the contemplation of suicide is serious, it's time to talk to someone that can relate to my issues. I grab my cellphone and immediately begin dialing, hoping he answers.

"Hello," he says. I'm relieved not to have gotten his voicemail.

"Hey Kendrick," I murmur. "How are you?"

"I'm good T. What's up with you? Everything okay?"

"Uh….I'm okay," I lie. "What are you up to?"

"Not much," he replies. "I'm watching a little TV, trying to figure out what I'm going to eat for dinner. Anyways, it's seven on a Sunday. Aren't you supposed to be at choir rehearsal?"

"Yeah, but I still don't feel like going out much. Although, I'm hungry too. You want to run with me to The Green Tortilla?"

"Yeah sure," he answers. "Just give me ten minutes."

"Alright, I'll come get you in ten," I respond. My plan is to go with Kendrick to grab some food, and perhaps go back to his place or come back to mine to talk. I prefer to go to his spot because he now lives in a single apartment on campus, which would be better for purposes of privacy. I don't want to risk anyone overhearing our conversation, and Carter will probably be back in our apartment any minute.

****

"Have a seat, I'm going to run into my room to get my phone charger," Kendrick says as we walk into his place. Thankfully, my plan to talk to him is playing out as I envisioned it.

"Okay Ken!" While he's grabbing his charger, I'm preparing to have this conversation.

"So T, I'm glad you called me to get some food, but what's up with you? I can tell something is off." He's now heading back into the living room to join me.

"Actually, I'm not doing that great," I confess. He then turns to face me looking concerned.

"Well what's wrong?" he further inquires. "Talk to me."

"I don't know where to start, but here it goes," I mumble. "I've been trying to figure out who I am sexually, but I can't help but feel like I'm drowning in my own thoughts." As I try to explain to Kendrick everything going on with me, I start to break down and cry. "Every time I weigh the pros and cons of being gay, it's like I'm literally under water and unable to breathe. I can't keep living like this. Hell, right before I called you, I actually typed up a suicide note. I wanted to die."

"I didn't know things had gotten this bad," he sighs as he hands me a box of tissue. "I'm glad you came to me before you did something permanent." I frantically try to regain control of my emotions.

"Ken, I have no clue what I'm supposed to do. I thought if I talked to you, that maybe you could help me through this."

"I'm definitely going to do what I can," he promises. "I think it's time I explain to you the real reason why I transferred to Hamilton." As weird as it sounds, Kendrick never told me why he transferred, and I can't recall me asking why either.

"Oh okay," I whisper.

"When I first got to Baldwin Locke University my freshman year, I decided to explore my sexuality. Up until that point, I like you felt that I may not like girls in the way I should, but had downplayed my gayness. While exploring, I met this guy named Xavier. He was a freshman as well at the time, but he was already secure with who he was. Because of his confidence, he wasn't concerned about PDA, and what people would think. So, he would try to hug or kiss me all out in the open. Since I was really insecure about who I was at the time, I hated that he was so expressive in front of folks. On the flip side of things, I'm sure he hated my need to keep everything private."

"Well, one day after a year of dating, Xavier attempted to kiss me in the stairwell leading to the campus computer lab, and someone spotted us. When I saw the spectator, I pushed Xavier off of me and yelled at him. I believe I told him to get the hell off me, and that I wasn't gay. I then ran out of the stairwell and left him there."

"What happened after that?" I interrupted. "Weren't his feelings hurt?" I'm hanging onto every word coming out of Kendrick's mouth.

"Xavier didn't take that public rejection well," he continued. "Later on that night, he sent me a text ending things between us. Then to make matters worse, the person that caught Xavier trying to kiss me was the campus gossip. This person managed to get the word spread around campus that I like men. When all this went down it was in the beginning of my sophomore year. And from that moment up until the point I transferred, I became an outcast on campus. The straight guy friends I had freshman year, no longer talked to me. I think they feared people would assume they were gay if they continued hanging out the new homo on campus. Plus the girls at school looked at me like I was Satan or something. It was as if I had betrayed them somehow. To top it all off, every now and then I would hear someone say something ignorant like 'look, there's the tall fag!'"

"Oh man really," I gasp. I was not expecting this backstory. Never would I have guessed that college educated people could be so hateful.

"Yep," he confirms. "But let me finish. Feeling like a social reject, I began to think maybe this was God telling me that he didn't approve of my choices. Like God was punishing me for being gay. Although I too read verses in the Bible condemning homosexuality, I pursued my feelings of wanting to be the true Kendrick. And unfortunately, I sensed I was paying for my choice. Because I thought both God and man turned their back on me, I allowed the devil to convince me that it would be better if I just peaced out on life."

"How did you decide not to do it?" I inquire. "And how did you cope with being you? The black gay you."

"Welp, prayer and really taking the time to think got me through that part of my life," he responds. "I tried praying that God would take the gay away. However, after a while I begin to think that praying that prayer was the equivalent of asking God to turn my brown eyes blue, or asking that He never let me grow grey hair. Tristan, we are made the way we are made. Just like I could get contacts to change my eye color, and dye to cover up the greys, I could tell myself I'm not gay and get a girlfriend or two. But at the end of the day, doing all of that just hides the person I was created to be."

Hearing Kendrick explain homosexuality in this way makes me look at being gay from a new perspective. I mean have I naively been praying that God change a trait in me that I've been born with?

"So once I began looking at my sexuality as something that's a natural part of me," Kendrick continues. "I started thinking that the social rejection was not a sign God turned his back on me, but more so that people in life can ignorant and cruel. Praying some more and referring to the Bible, I concluded that God loves me T. His love for me, and for you, is unconditional. And I love Him beyond words. That love between Him and I is the foundation for our relationship. It's this shared adoration in our relationship that lets me know God hasn't kicked me to the curb." He slightly chuckles.

To say that I'm impressed by Kendrick's recap of acceptance would be an understatement. His story is persuading me to embrace my true sexual orientation, rather than continuously shy from it. In addition, his ability to unify his sexuality and religion is inspiration for my own unification process. I'm starting to have hope that I can finally let go of the guilt and shame I've been carrying.

"Ken, thank you again for coming to the rescue. Had you not answered when I called..." I'm more than appreciative of him being here for me. For the first time in a long time, I don't feel like I'm sinking but slowly coming up for air.

"Let me stop you right there," he chimes in. "I'm the one that's thankful. I, along with everyone you know, would have been devastated had something happened to you. And I'm not saying my understanding of all this is the absolute right one, but it's the one I've arrived at. I know you've already been praying, but I encourage you to continue to do so. You'll figure it all out. Oh, and please make sure you stay away from that dark place. Suicide is never the answer."

"Okay gotcha," I agree. "So whatever happened to Xavier?"

"Well I tried to reach out to him T. I wanted to apologize, and I thought maybe he could look past what I did and be a friend when I was going through my mini breakdown. But he never returned any of my calls. When I saw him around campus, he pretended not to even see me. I felt some type of way about it at first, but then I found out that he was bashing me in some online gay chat groups. So I'm good on never talking to Xavier again."

"Damn Ken," I sigh. "What was he saying?" Curiosity forced me to ask.

"Things like people should stay away from me because I'm an ignorant closeted gay with a small penis. He also said some other petty stuff that were lies and aren't important."

"Having been up and close to it, I assure you that no part of you is small," I chuckle. He gives me a shove and laughs with me. Emotionally drained for the night, I have to talk about something a little less heavy. "So you know my Cavs are looking good. I think they may actually win a title this season?"

"Yeah you hold out for that title," Kendrick sarcastically replies.

November 6, 2008 (Thursday)

  Having done some talking with the Lord and soul searching these past few days, I've finally arrived at a place of much needed peace. I stopped trying to fight the inevitable, and came to terms with the fact that I'm a black man that happens to be attracted to other men. Also, I started believing that just because I like men doesn't make me any less of a Christian. My relationship with Christ is bigger than my sexual preference. Although I haven't figured out yet how I would come out of the proverbial closet to those closest to me, I'm proud to have at least taken this first step of self-acceptance.

  In my first act as an *official* gay man, I contacted Kendrick yesterday. I want to explore the territory beyond friendship with him, and decided the best way to do that is to go on a date. So last night, I asked if he was free to meet up tonight for dinner; thankfully, he said yes. Even though I want this dinner date to occur, I'm kind of apprehensive about going to a restaurant just the two of us. We have been to places just the two of us before, but for some reason I feel that if we were seen together in public now, people would assume we are dating. While I accept who I am, I'm not ready to see if the general masses are willing to do the same quite yet. For that reason, I proposed going to his place and making him dinner. Plus, I figured he would appreciate me cooking him a meal, since I never did when he walked me back to my apartment after my trial run with liquor. With a game plan for tonight set in motion, I'm excitedly headed to Ken's.

****

  As I knock on his front door, I try my best to shake off last minute jitters. It's crazy. Kendrick and I have seen each other naked, been physical, and known each other for over a year; and yet, I'm nervous. I guess I'm a little worried that him seeing me at my lowest point, has somehow tainted how he feels about me.

"Hey T, how are ya?" Kendrick greets. It's show time.

"I'm good Ken. I'm ready to do some flexing in this kitchen." As we snicker, I step into his apartment and he closes the door. We then embrace each other in a hug. I don't know how he always smells so good. And my gosh, something about being in his strong arms makes me want to melt like butter. Stepping back from Kendrick, I take a closer look at his date attire. He has on this light grey long sleeve Henley shirt that hugs every contour of his arms, and squeezes his chest just right. On the bottom, he's wearing dark indigo blue jeans that seem to fit him perfectly around his thighs before bunching slightly as they fell on his wheat Timberland boots. Man he looks good.

"Oh, well we'll see about that Chef Boyardee," he jokes.

"Yes you will see," I quip. "Just go and have a seat on your couch, and let me do my thang." I say this as if my name is on the lease.

"Alright T," Kendrick smiles. He proceeds to grab his TV remote and a spot on his sofa. I head to the kitchen and begin unpacking the groceries I brought to cook. I want to hurry and finish this meal, because I don't want to spend all evening over a stove. For dinner I'm preparing a strawberry spinach salad with candied pecans, and shrimp linguine Alfredo. Since I've made this meal a few times before, it should take me no longer than thirty-five minutes or so to whip it up. Now once I find the pots, pans, and cooking utensils in here, I'll be in business.

****

"Okay, dinner is served," I announce as I finish placing the food on the table.

"Good, because I'm hungry," he responds. He turns his TV off, and instead of coming toward the dinner table to join me, he walks back to his bedroom.

"Um Ken, where are you going?"

"Gonna grab my mini-speaker real quick so I can play some music while we eat." Music during dinner is an excellent idea. I should've thought of that. And I wish I was twenty-one so I could have bought some wine for the occasion; but since I'm not, I hope the apple cider I purchased will suffice.

Coming out of his room, I see Kendrick eye the dinner table, then me. It's funny how his face is saying a thousand words, yet his lips never part.

"Wow T," he exclaims. "This looks amazing! You did this for me?"

"Yeah," I confidently answer. "But I did it for me too! A brotha gotta eat." We both just chuckle. After he gets things situated with the music, he joins me at the dinner table.

"Well let's eat," he says. Kendrick blesses the food, and then takes his first bite. "T, if I hadn't seen you with my own two eyes, I wouldn't believe you prepared this. I mean this pasta is restaurant quality. I'm impressed!" Hearing the compliment reaffirms what I already know. I'm skilled in the kitchen.

"Ha thanks Ken. I'm glad you like it."

"Oh definitely," he reaffirms. "Now you're definitely going to have to make me that breakfast I never got."

"Oh is that right?" I rhetorically ask. "I think next time you have to cook for me."

"Okay bet," he counters. "What kind of Top Ramen do you prefer? Chicken or shrimp?" I'm unable to contain my laughter. I know Kendrick's not an executive chef at a five star restaurant, but offering me my choice of Oodles of Noodles is too funny to be taken seriously.

"Really fool?" I quip while smiling. "I'll pass on the Ramen, but thanks for the offer."

"Man, you're missing out," he jokes.

"Moving on," I insist. "Did David send you a text today about wanting to bring a new line of guys into Beta next semester?"

"He sure did," Kendrick replies. "I told him I would be cool with it, but that I wouldn't be too involved with the process. Next semester is my last semester in college, and I'm trying to finish undergrad on a high note with no problems."

"I get that," I respond. I understand how time consuming helping guys become new members of the fraternity can be. The process has a tendency of distracting you from academics if you're not careful.

"I plan to be around the new guys just long enough for them to know who I am," he continues. "And speaking of the text, did you read the list of names he had in mind?"

"Yep," I tell him. "From the ones I know on it, I think it's a good group of guys. What do you think?

"It is a good group," Kendrick seconds. "There was one name on the list that stuck out to me though. That Tyson kid, he's a freshman right?"

"Um yeah he is," I confirm. I don't know too much about Tyson. I just know he's a freshman at Hamilton from Tallahassee, Florida. He had been at a study hall session from what I hear. Due to my self-exploration phase I went through, I didn't attend too many of those this fall. However, I crossed paths with him around campus, and I met him at the first BSAS meeting of the school year. He's a short slim guy. He looks to be both black and of Asian heritage. I also know that Tyson is very well put together. Every time I saw him, he had a cleanly shaven face, fresh shape-up, and an outfit that made him look "modelesque." All in all, he's a pretty handsome kid.

"I thought so," Kendrick said. "I think he will be an interesting one to bring into the fold."

"What do you mean by 'interesting' Ken?"

"I'll explain more, once I get to know him better," he replies.

"Hmm....alrighty then," I mumble. I want to know what he means right now, but I'll wait for later to come. I move the conversation along, and we continue eating and enjoying the night.

****

Now that we both finished dinner, I get up to clear the dishes off the table. However, as I reach for Kendrick's plates, he grabs my arm.

"T, what do you think you're doing?"

"What you mean Ken? I'm cleaning up. The table won't clean itself."

"I know that smart ass," he chuckles. "But I'll worry about that stuff in a few. Come join me over here on the sofa and watch a movie with me. I scooped something up from the Redbox."

"Cool, I guess I can do that," I submit. He lets go of my arm, and we both walk to the couch. Since his sofa is really more of a loveseat, when we sit down our legs slightly brush up against each other.

"I rented one of my favorite movies," Kendrick says. "I rented *Harlem Nights* with Eddie Murphy. Have you seen it?" I'm pretty sure I've heard of it, but I know for certain I haven't seen it.

"Nope," I respond. "So it will be my first time."

"Oh well you're about to enjoy this then," he assures. He powers on the TV and cues up the DVD player. But then he abruptly stands up.

"Everything alright," I inquire.

"I'm just turning off the light so there isn't a glare on the TV."

"Oh okay," I state.

When he sits back down, he manages to get even closer to me than before. He throws his right arm around me, and pulls me tighter into his body. Since he is obviously trying to get cozy with me, I do my part and lay my head on his chest, nestling right under his chin. It's so nice to be here with Kendrick like this. So nice in fact, that I slowly stop paying attention to the movie. Thinking about how I'm finally able to be with him like this without a guilty conscious, is purely amazing.

"T, you didn't think that was funny?"

"Huh?" I whisper.

"Are you paying attention to the movie?" he asks. "That thing Eddie Murphy just said is one of the funniest parts."

"My bad," I apologize. "I guess I zoned out."

"Well stop that, and watch," he demands with the biggest grin on his face. Kendrick starts rubbing the back of my head with his giant right hand. If he thought rubbing my head was going to get me to pay attention, he couldn't be more wrong. Him caressing me like this is further distracting me. Acting on impulse, I take my left hand and slide it back and forth on his thigh. With my palm motioning up and down his leg, I notice a bulge start to form in the seat of his jeans.

"Ken, is the movie that exciting for you?" I tease.

"You think you're funny don't you," he scoffs. "You know what you're doing."

"Nope, I'm innocent over here." I'm playing coy.

"You're innocent over there, huh T? We will see about that." He pulls me into him, and like two magnets our lips embrace. His mouth is just as sweet as I remember it. And he is sucking on my bottom lip, which I've found to be the biggest turn on. I have no idea how my heart is still beating, because I'm almost positive that all of my blood has raced to my loins.

Trying to get more comfortable, I swing my legs over the side of the love seat and lean further into Kendrick and this kiss. His hand that was gripping my head, is now moving down my back pulling at my sweater. I take this as a sign, so I pull away from him just long enough to remove it. Shirtless and feeling the passion of the moment, I again change my position. I quickly mount him. I'm straddling him as if he's my horse. He must like this new position, because the way he is now interacting with me can only be described as animalistic ecstasy. I know this is going to be the perfect ending to our perfect first date.

Chapter 6: Spring 2009

January 19, 2009 (Monday)

  I am beyond thrilled for the start of this semester. I'm in such a great place in my life. Academically speaking, things are great. In spite of my "identity crisis," I somehow managed to get an A in all of my classes last semester. I look forward to keeping up this trend. In terms of work, I was recently promoted to the supervisor position. My now former boss Stephanie had graduated and left Hamilton at the end of the fall semester, and I was chosen a week ago to be her replacement. I'm excited about the opportunity, and the more money it brings along with it.

  Adding to my joyous mood this spring is my personal life. Things between Kendrick and I couldn't be more amazing. We've been dating for about two months, and each day we appear to be growing closer and closer. I've made a habit of going to his apartment whenever I can, just to spend time with him. Since we're both discreet about our private lives, his apartment and mine (when Carter isn't present) are the only places we can regularly go to be ourselves and fully enjoy each other's company.

  The only thing bothering me a little these days is my relationship with Denise. We haven't been hanging out like we used to since I spend most of my free time with Kendrick. Plus, I've been a little unsure about how to feel knowing I'm dating someone Denise had a crush on. I once felt guilty about it, but I've moved passed that. Heck, I'm actually saving her some possible heartache and embarrassment. And it's not like she was in a relationship with him at any point, nor could she ever be. It's with this newfound rationale, and the fact I'm missing my good friend, that I called her a few days ago. I wanted to schedule a little time with Denise for lunch. Since she just came back to campus yesterday from a month at home for the winter break, we chose to go out today on the MLK holiday. I'm currently searching my closest to find something to wear so I can go meet her within the hour.

****

"Denise, what up home skillet?" I jokingly greet as I enter her student apartment.

"What up fool?" she responds as she hugs me. "I'll be ready in five minutes."

"Okay cool, no rush," I say. It's funny to see her frantically walk around the apartment looking for shoes to put on, and a comb to run through her hair. As she attempts to finish getting ready, I decide I would share some big news with her. The news is guaranteed to blow her mind. I know it will because it blew my mind when my mom told me yesterday.

"Hey Denise," I begin. "I know you're getting ready, but can you stop for a moment and listen to me? Got something to tell you." She then comes out of the bathroom and walks into the living room where I'm standing. She's looking at me with a comb still in her hair. "Well, I know I've been slacking as a friend lately, and I'd like to make it up to you."

"Yes you have, but I forgive you," she giggles.

"Ha, why thank you," I continue. "Well last night, my mom told me she was able to get a hold of four tickets to the Neighborhood Inaugural Ball. She, being the loving and sweet lady that she is, gave me two of the tickets. Obviously one of the tickets is for me. The other one is for my date."

"Hold up," she interjects. "Do you mean tickets for a real inaugural ball? As in for Barack Obama?"

"Yes," I confirm.

"Tristan that's fantastic news! You know how hard it is to get tickets for anything related to this inauguration? You're about to have an amazing time. Heck you're about to be a part of history."

"We're about to have an amazing time," I tell her.

"What do you mean?" she questions, as an anticipatory expression of nervousness consumes her face. Denise looks like she has a lottery ticket, and is waiting for me to call her winning numbers.

"Denise, you get a ticket!" I tried to deliver the surprise news as if I was Oprah Winfrey giving away a car.

"Boy don't say it, if you don't mean it!"

"I mean it," I chuckle.

"I can't believe this," she screams. She starts jumping up and down in excitement. "Like how is this all happening? Did your mom have to buy tickets? Should I be paying her for it?"

"Don't worry about the how. Just be thankful like I am that it's happening. And there is no need to pay my mother anything. She got the tickets as a gift from a former associate that used to work with her."

"Oh my gosh this is so exciting Tristan! I gotta call mama and daddy, and tell them I'm gonna to be partying with the Obamas!" I can't help but laugh at my friend. In all the commotion, her southern twang became a bit more prominent.

"Yes, you go ahead and do that," I tell her.

"Before I call my mama, I have to ask one more question. Why are you taking me and not Mercedes?"

"Mercedes and I aren't talking like that these days," I share. "We both realized that the reason we couldn't commit to a relationship, is because it wasn't meant to be."

"I'm sorry to hear that," she sighs.

"I'm fine, trust me," I tell her. "It truly was a mutual decision."

"Okay just asking," she responds. "Now back to this call." Denise pulls her phone off its charger and dials. "Mama, guess where your baby gets to go tomorrow…"

While she gives the inaugural news to her family back home, I pull out my own phone to text Kendrick. I want to tell him how Denise reacted when she found out she has a ticket. Thankfully, he didn't mind that I gave Denise my extra inaugural ball ticket. He wouldn't be able to go even if I had offered the opportunity. His boss at his new internship is hosting an inaugural celebration at her home, and he felt obligated to attend. There is a full-time job opening up in his office soon, and he's trying to do everything he can to make sure he gets it. Plus, my mom gave me the extra ticket under the guise that I bring a female companion. Kendrick and I may be an item now, but by no means am I ready to introduce him to my mom in a partner capacity.

"Alright Tristan, you ready?" Being the multi-tasker that she is, she finished combing her hair and putting on her shoes, all while wrapping things up with her parents.

"Yep," I answer. "Let's go get something to eat. I'm hungry."

"Food we can definitely do," she agrees. "But a good friend will take me shopping after we eat. I've got to find something to wear for tomorrow. Mama is putting some money in my bank account to get a new dress, so we have to make sure we get to the stores. She told me, 'my baby has to look good if she is going to be that close to our new president.' By the way, she said she loves you even more."

"Deal," I second. "Just promise me we won't be at the mall until it closes."

"I'd love to promise you that Tristan, but you can't rush fashion. I've got to pick the right dress that will make my parents proud, but at the same time will have a single man ready to beg for my number." My friend is still funny and crazy.

January 20, 2009 (Tuesday)

"Tristan I'm still shocked that we're here," Denise whispers as she leans into me. "I never imagined that I'd be at an inaugural ball for America's first black president. This is just crazy."

"I feel you on that," I respond. "We are literally taking part in a historic moment. Do you want me to take a picture of you with your phone so you can send it to your family?"

"That would be great thanks." Denise hands me her phone and then gets into her semi-prom girl pose. I take picture after picture as she makes subtle changes. "Can you take one more?"

"Sure," I agree. While taking the last photo, I hear a familiar voice approaching me.

"Tristan, go stand next to Denise and I'll take your picture together." Turning around, I see my mom and her special friend Henry. I'm not particularly fond of Henry, but he appears to make my mom happy, so I've learned to tolerate his presence.

"Okay Mom thanks." I stand next to Denise, officially completing the standard prom portrait.

"Say cheese you two," my mom requests. I'm slightly embarrassed by her use of such a cliché photographer expression.

"Thank you Ms. Steele," Denise says as she reaches out to collect her phone. "And thank you again for the ticket. I don't know how to ever repay you."

"Oh please," my mom exclaims. "Your gratitude is good enough. You and Tristan have fun tonight. Now

Denise, if you wouldn't mind letting me borrow my son for two minutes before you all have too much fun."

"Of course," Denise replies. I walk with my mom about fifteen feet away from Denise and Henry. Knowing my mom, she is probably going grill me about why I'm not dating Denise. After meeting Denise a few times, my mother has grown quite fond of her. She has hinted more than once that Denise and I should be more than friends.

"My baby looks so handsome tonight," my mom starts. "Now do yourself a favor and make that Denise your girlfriend before some other boy comes and scoops her up." And there it is. She's not even subtle today.

"Mom, I told you we are just friends," I reaffirm. "Trying to date Denise would be like trying to be with my sister if I had one."

"Mmhmm," my mom scoffs. "Well your 'sister' would make a good match for you; but I won't push the issue. Let's go back over to our dates, they look bored to tears." It's true. Denise and Henry are just standing there. They aren't even talking to each other.

"Henry, you feel like dancing or what," my mom asks as we return to our plus ones. He grabs her hand and leads her to the dance floor. "Tristan and Denise, I'll see you later."

"See you," Denise giggles. Once my mom and Henry leave, Denise shoots me this concerned look. "Is everything alright? Did I do something to offend your mama?"

"Absolutely not," I reply. "Trust me, my mom likes you. She just wanted to give me some advice."

"That's good to hear," she sighs with relief. "But ooo, do you hear that?

"Hear what," I inquire.

"They are playing my song." As I listen to the music, I realize the song playing is "Brick House" by the Commodores. "Time to follow your mama to the dance floor. Let's go!"

****

After two hours of the inaugural festivities, I'm kind of ready to go. The excitement of the event is wearing off a bit, and my so-called date is trying to land a real one. For the past thirty minutes, Denise has been conversing with this guy named Rob. On the surface Rob appears to be a good guy. He's a little over six foot, lanky, well groomed, and pretty attractive. I could be wrong, but he looks to be Latino. Denise and I met him at the bar when we were getting something to drink. I can tell he found her attractive so I excused myself from the mix so they could get to know each other a little bit. I'm just waiting for her to rejoin me. I don't mind waiting though, I'm happy to see her hit it off with someone. However, since I'm over here just chilling, I might as well text Kendrick. I know he's at a function of his own, but I hope he responds.

Me: Hey Ken! How's it going?

Kendrick: It's going good T. I'm just ready to go. Most of the people here are old enough to be my mother and father.

Me: I'm ready to go too! Don't get me wrong. I'm so thankful for the chance to be here, but I got to get out of these clothes and relax.

Kendrick: I get it. What you doin when you get back to campus?

> *Me: Idk. I was planning to drop Denise off at her apartment, and then head to my apartment to change clothes. Then maybe I'll come swing by your place. That is if you are going to be back on campus, and want some company.*

Kendrick: I'm always up for hanging with you. I should be back at my apartment in about an hour.

> *Me: Ok bet. See you soon!*

Peaking up from my phone, I see Denise approaching. She is grinning from ear to ear, so I assume she was thoroughly impressed by Rob.

"Sorry I was gone for so long," she apologizes while still smiling.

"No need to be sorry," I respond. "How did it go over there with him?"

"Tristan, it went so well, and you better be glad it did. I wanted to kill you for leaving me over there with him by myself. But from talking with him, I found out Rob is in his first year of med school at George Washington University."

"Oh a future doctor," I mock. "Did you get them digits, or at least give him some?"

"As a matter of fact fool, I did give him my number," she retorts.

"Well watch out there now! My sister from another mister is about to land her a boo thang!"

"Tristan, shut up! Don't jinx me." We both erupt into laughter.

"Ha, sorry Denise. But hey, you about ready to leave?"

"I've seen the president, took pictures for the family, and got a boy's number, so yes," she answers. "We can roll on out."

"Great. Let's go find my mom and say goodbye, then we can head back to campus."

January 26, 2009 (Monday)

Tonight my fraternity brothers and I have a meeting to discuss the guys that would potentially pledge Mu Theta this semester. Since I've had another long day, I don't really feel like going to a meeting; but, I know I have to go. Hopefully the discussion will last no longer than an hour. I'm just glad the meeting is at Chance's apartment, who happens to live in the same building I do, two floors below me. Having knocked on his door already, I'm just waiting for Chance to open it and let me in.

"Hey Tristan, come on in," Chance greets. Entering his apartment, I'm shocked to see that Randy, David, and Lamont are sitting in the living room. Usually, these three are the last ones to show up for everything.

"What are you three doing here so early?" I question.

"Wow Tristan, we can't even get a hello first," David scoffs.

"My b, hello," I tell them. "It's just that I'm surprised you guys beat me here."

"Well they say there is a first time for everything man," Randy jokes. "Besides, we all went to eat at The Lighthouse before this, and then followed Chance back here." Part of me feels some type of way because they went without me. I've been wanting to eat at The Lighthouse since it opened up on campus at the start of the semester. However, I suspect I didn't get an invite because David knew I got out of my last class only ten minutes ago.

"Alright cool," I respond. "So I guess we are just waiting on Willie, James, and Kendrick." My line brother Brian graduated last spring and moved away to New York, so he wouldn't be joining us. Gavin, Marcus, and Arlen also wouldn't be coming. They were taking less active roles in undergraduate affairs since they now feel the Mu Theta chapter has enough young brothers in it to effectively run things.

"Kendrick," Lamont gasps. "I thought he didn't want to be involved with the process this time."

"Naw man," I begin correcting Lamont. "He wants to be involved, but not to the extent he was last time. He told me he is trying to graduate without any problems."

"Ohhhh," Lamont sighs. "I was looking at him sideways then for no reason. I thought he didn't want to be bothered at all. Chance and I are both graduating this semester too, and I couldn't understand why Kendrick was trying to skip out on bringing in some new boys if we weren't. He's just taking a little bit of a back seat with me this go around. I get it."

"Yeah a back seat," I repeat. Honestly, if I were Kendrick and working an internship that's leading to a career and planning on graduating this semester, I may be completely removed from the pledge process altogether. But that's just me.

"While we're waiting on the other fellas, why don't you tell us how you dropped the ball with Mercedes," Randy proposes. I'm a little thrown off by his inquisition.

"Say what now?" I exclaim.

"Man you heard him," David adds. "We saw her hugging up with that boy Jackson from the baseball team. So, what happened with you two?"

"If y'all must know, we talked and realized we're just better as friends." I stop speaking and notice the stares from around the room. They are looking at me as if I said something wrong.

"Forget all that," Lamont chimes in. "Did you get some from her or not?" I can't say that I'm stunned by his bluntness. He, along with the rest of my brothers, know me to still be a virgin, and they've been eagerly awaiting for my so called *cherry* to be popped. What they don't know however, is that Kendrick has already without question stripped me of my V card.

"Naw I didn't," I answer. I refuse to be like those guys that lie about their sexual endeavors to impress their friends, so I just state the truth.

"Damn Tristan, you blew it," Randy asserts. I'm not a fan of being put on the spot like this, and really wish we could move on. Suddenly, there's a knock on Chance's front door. As Chance opens it, I'm glad to see Kendrick. It's like he sensed my uncomfortably and came to my rescue.

"What's going on bruhs?" Kendrick calls out, entering the apartment. After dapping up my other fraternity brothers, he sits in the seat directly across from me. Unfortunately, before Chance has the opportunity to get settled back in his seat, there's another knock at the door.

"Can't you all just come at one time next time," Chance jokes. "I'm tired of getting up." Everyone chuckles. Fortunately for him, he shouldn't have to open the door any more tonight because he opens the door to Willie and James.

"Since everyone is here, I'll just go ahead and jump right in," David says as he whips out a sheet of paper. "I'll just go down the list of names I have here, and we can discuss each one in terms of membership this semester. First up is that sophomore Victor Parker."

"Which one is he?" James asks.

"You know," David answers. "The dude on the track team with the baby fro."

"Oh that guy," James replies. "From what I know he's cool people. And he is on the track team, so that will be a good look for our chapter."

"Yeah, plus he comes out to our events when he can," Chance adds. We all seem to agree on Victor, and move our way down David's list.

One by one David reads off the names of the Beta Kappa Nu prospects. As a collective group, we agree on everyone so far. I'm thrilled with how quickly this going. Hopefully this means the meeting will conclude sooner than I thought. There is just one more guy we have to discuss.

"Now how do you guys feel about the freshman Tyson Williams," David inquires. "He's been to our events, finished last semester with great grades, and I know a lot of freshmen know him and like him. He's also in BSAS with Tristan." Because David mentions me in this regard, I feel compelled to give my input.

"I think we should let him join," I recommend. "From what I hear, he's been putting in a lot of work for BSAS for the Black History Month programs. Our chapter always needs people willing to work. Also, I spoke to him after the BSAS meeting this past Thursday and I found out his dad pledged Beta Kappa Nu in the spring of '85 at Delaware State. Tyson said his dad really made him want to be a Beta man."

"Okay so Tristan likes him, what about the rest of you," David queries.

"I don't know about the kid," Lamont inserts.

"Why what's up?" David probes. "What don't you know about him?"

"I'm just gonna say it," Lamont counters. "That boy seems real fruity to me. The way he dresses and acts makes me think he's soft. I don't want him representing our chapter." I know Lamont's not necessarily a proponent of homosexuality, but I didn't expect this to come out of his mouth.

"Yeah, I think ole boy is definitely a homo," Willie seconds. "That freshman girl I was messing with lives next door to him, and she told me he always has this one dude going into his room at night." I can't help but think of my own nighttime visits to Kendrick's place. I hope there aren't nosey ass folks tracking my movements or Kendrick's.

"Um, how do you know that's not Tyson's roommate?" Chance asks.

"Because this boy lives in one of those single dorms," Willie states. "He has no roommate. I'm telling you, he's gay."

"So if it turns out that Tyson is gay, then what does that mean?" Kendrick questions. "We can't accept him into the chapter and fraternity if he is gay?" I've developed a knack for sensing when Kendrick is agitated, and it's clear to me that he's becoming just that.

"Hell no, he can't be in this chapter," Lamont shoots back. "I don't want people saying that this is 'the gay frat.' I don't know about y'all, but I don't want people thinking I like it in the ass because of one nigga."

"Well damn," Kendrick exclaims. "I thought we were a fraternity that embraced all mankind, not just the straight ones. We can't deny a good guy membership based on what he may or may not do in the privacy of his own bedroom."

"Kendrick," Lamont rudely interrupts. "We are supposed to protect the reputation of Beta Kappa Nu. How can we say that we are doing that, letting Tyson and people like him into our fraternity?" To say I'm dumbfounded is a complete understatement. My line brother is coming off as a homophobic bigot right now.

"Are you serious Lamont?" Kendrick huffs, while looking disgusted. "So you don't want to be known as a gay fraternity, but you rather be known as a prejudice one?"

"Why are you battling so hard for this guy?" Willie intervenes. "Are you gay or something?" Nervous about how Kendrick will respond, I know I've got to slide into the conversation.

"Whoa," I yell. "Everybody just calm down! We are all brothers here, and there is no need for people to get upset or to make accusations. Willie and Lamont, I think Kendrick was trying to make you aware that what you're suggesting is discrimination. What kind of reputation would that leave the chapter with?" I'm hoping the other brothers in the room will chime in here to back me up. Unfortunately, they just seem to be spectators of this debate.

"Whatever Tristan," Willie grunts. "Let's just vote on this guy so we can stop talking about it. I'm voting no on this boy."

"Me too," Lamont seconds. Up until this point, my chapter really hadn't experienced such a divide in opinion. Every chapter decision made has surprisingly been made unanimously. However according to our chapter's bylaws, complete unanimity is not needed in order for the chapter to proceed with something. What is needed, is a simple majority consensus of the current active members. So in fact, Tyson could become a member of Beta Kappa Nu without Willie and Lamont's approval.

"Alright then," Kendrick says. "There are two votes no. What do you think Randy?" Randy is a guy that hates conflict. He usually did or said anything he could to avoid it.

"I guess I will vote no too," Randy mumbles, barely audible. "I'd rather not bring someone into the chapter that current brothers dislike this much. I don't want anything to mess up the good vibe we have with each other." Randy's vote and reasoning for the vote are definitely reflective of his Kumbaya attitude.

"Got it," Kendrick replies. "What about you Chance?" Chance I assume would vote in favor of Tyson, because he is a peer diversity counselor. So one's sexuality shouldn't matter to him.

"Tyson has my blessing," Chance votes. "Who am I to discriminate? Especially based on unproven speculation and rumors?"

"Great," Kendrick responds. He's clearly pleased with Chance's decision. "Tristan, can I safely assume that you're in favor of Tyson?"

"Yeah Ken," I answer. I felt obligated to vote for Tyson, because it's the right thing to do. Lamont and Willie have no valid reason to reject his request for membership.

"Only James and David are left then," Kendrick continues. It's funny how Kendrick has seemingly taken over this meeting from David. I guess it's his right to do so as chapter president. "What do you guys think?"

"I mean it's not like the kid is walking around the campus in women's clothes or something if he is gay," James begins. "So I think it will be fine if we let him in." The pro Tyson side of this vote now has enough people on it to allow the freshman the opportunity to become a Beta. Even if David votes against him, it won't matter. In the case of a tie, the president of the chapter gets to make the final decision. Since Kendrick is the president, and he already expressed how he feels about Willie and Randy's attempt at exclusion, Tyson pledging this semester is a done deal.

"And I agree with James," David concurs. "Let the dude go ahead and pledge."

"There you have it," Kendrick says. "Looks like Tyson will join the other boys on line in a few days." Although Kendrick is beaming with happiness, Willie and Randy are seething.

"If y'all want this boy to be a Beta so bad, just know I'm not going to have anything to do with making that happen," Willie announces.

"Yeah," Lamont blurts out. "I'm not going to sit here and support this bullshit. I'm not going to help y'all destroy this chapter's reputation." Before any of us could attempt to talk to our disgruntled brothers and convince them to change their minds, they abruptly get up and leave.

"They'll come around," Chance mutters. "Hopefully."

February 3, 2009 (Tuesday)

A little over a week has gone by, and my chapter of fraternity brothers is still in an unusual state of discord. Mu Theta has been divided into two different factions. One faction consists of Kendrick, Chance, James, David, and I. Basically, the brothers that support Tyson becoming a member of Beta Kappa Nu. On the other side of the divide is Lamont and Willie, who staunchly oppose Tyson's membership. Although Randy voted with Lamont and Willie, he opted to remain as neutral as possible in all of this and not take sides.

It doesn't feel right bringing a new group of guys into a brotherhood that isn't quite so brotherly at the moment. However, our chapter is preparing to lose three of our eight members due to graduation at the end of this semester, so each of us knows the importance of cultivating new Beta men. I only hope the eight of us come together soon and get pass this drama before adding new personalities to the mix.

Trying to expedite this reunification process, I invited both Lamont and Willie over to my place thinking we could resolve things. Unfortunately, they both declined my invitation. I even attempted to get them to meet up with me and the rest of the chapter for dinner at The Lighthouse; but, the two of them made up a reason as to why they couldn't make it. My other brothers, minus Kendrick, tried to mend fences with Lamont and Willie as well, but, nothing was working up until this point.

Then out of the blue around noon today, I received a mass text message from our older brother Marcus. It basically stated that the anti-Tyson faction had spoken to him and told him about the issues we were having lately. He requested that we meet up at his place if we are free around eight tonight. I'm not sure what Marcus could say to fix our problem, but most

Majoring in Me   183

of us agreed to meet. At the moment, Kendrick, Chance, James, and I are in the midst of driving to his home.

    "I'm telling y'all right now," Kendrick scoffs. "If tonight turns into a shouting match, I'm walking out of Marcus' house, and heading to the car." If he does wind up leaving, I'm not sure where he would go. I'm the one driving.

    "Bruh, let's try to go in this thing thinking positively," James says.

    "I'll try to," Kendrick responds.

    "Alright fellas we're here," I announce pulling into an open parking space near Marcus' townhome. As the four of us get out of my car and walk on the path to Marcus' place, I take out my phone to send Kendrick a message. Even though he is literally right beside me, I want to tell him something that I don't want Chance and James to hear.

> *Me: Hey babe, please go into this meeting with a leveled head. Remember we want to try to fix things, not make them worse.*

    I hear a bell sound from Kendrick's coat pocket. He looks down at his phone, and begins to smirk. I assume he received my text and is now reading it. While he appears to be typing away on his phone, James knocks as we arrive at the front door. Waiting on our big brother to answer and let us in, we all did what we could to stay warm in the freezing cold February air. I feel my phone vibrating in my hand, and open the message Kendrick just sent to me.

Kendrick: T I'm going to try to keep calm. If not for the sake of the chapter, at least for you since you

*asked. I hope I'm rewarded later
for not blowing up.* LOL ;-)

Me: Rewarded?!?

*Kendrick: Yeah rewarded! So make
sure you have that good lotion,
because I'm gonna want a good ole
foot massage.*

I uncontrollably burst into laughter. Kendrick knows I hate touching feet, so the idea of a foot massage is nothing but comical.

"Tristan, what's so funny?" Chance inquires.

"Um….nothing," I mumble. I slyly glance over at Kendrick and he is trying to mask his smile behind his hand. I shift my eyes to Marcus' front door as I hear it open up.

"Hey fellas, come on in," Marcus welcomes. James, Chance, Kendrick, and I walk into Marcus' house and head downstairs to his basement. Lamont, Randy, Willie, and David don't appear to be here yet. However, what is here are a few boxes of pizza. "So we are just waiting on the rest of the guys to show up. But while we wait, you guys help yourselves to some food." I didn't expect to be fed tonight, but since the pizza is here, I might as well have a slice or two.

"You don't have to tell me twice," James exclaims, bolting in the direction of the boxed spread.

****

About twenty minutes have gone by, and the rest of the chapter still hasn't arrived. James has now gone through half a box of pizza by himself. I ate my two slices, and I'm already getting the *itis*. If everyone else doesn't get here soon, I'm going to slowly slip into a nap. Before I close my eyelids too tight, the doorbell rings.

"That's probably the rest of the guys," Marcus says on his way up the stairs. I can hear him open the door and greet people as they enter his home. Marcus and his guests make their way back down to the basement, and I quickly realize that there are more people coming than I anticipated. Not only do Lamont, Willie, and Randy walk into the basement behind Marcus, but so do Arlen and Gavin. I wasn't aware that our other big brothers would be joining us, but perhaps it's for the best.

"Everybody's here but David," Marcus points out. "Does anyone know if he's coming?" Now that he mentions it, David isn't here and I've no clue if he plans on attending this impromptu gathering.

"David has a test tomorrow and said he had to study," Randy answers.

"Oh...," Marcus sighs. "I wanted everyone to be here, but we'll have to work with what we have. I asked Gavin and Arlen to join us, because I think they could give you guys some good advice. I briefly caught them up on everything going on based on what Willie and Lamont told me. I'll let Gavin and Arlen say what they want to say, I'll give my two cents, and then you young boys can talk so we can get this chapter back on track."

"Damn Marcus, I can't even get a slice of pizza first," Arlen jokes. "It's cool, I'll get something to eat in a minute. Before I give my input though, let me ask those of you who want this kid to be a member of Beta Kappa Nu a question. Why do you want him to join?" I for one am glad he asked this question, because I'm positive Lamont and Willie didn't share the positives about Tyson.

"Arlen, this is a good kid," Kendrick claims. "He is a second semester freshman with great grades. He's involved with BSAS with Tristan, and has been to several of our events on campus. Plus, he's wanted to be a Beta his whole life. Heck, his dad pledged Beta at Delaware State back in '85, so it's all he knows. I've got a gut feeling that the chapter really would benefit from having him."

"Oh so Tyson sounds like a good person to have on our side based on what you told me," Arlen deduces, sounding as if he's just heard these things for the first time. "Now that I have more of a complete picture, I'll say two things. First, it's important to have quality guys when bringing in new members. Like I said, Tyson sounds like good people. Second, it's also important to uphold the reputation of our chapter." I'm getting confused as to what Arlen is trying to tell us. I just want to know if he's team Tyson or not.

"The reputation of the Mu Theta chapter has always been a great one," Arlen continues. "We have always been known for throwing the best parties, hosting the most innovative community service events, and creating the most helpful on-campus programs for the students at Hamilton. To continue being known for such, we always recruit guys that we believe will be an asset in upholding this reputation." Arlen is now boring me with this monologue of his.

"Now what someone does sexually is none of the chapter's business," Arlen drags on. "But if what he does sexually can deter what you all as Betas try to accomplish on campus, then that may be a problem. So you young brothers have to think. Will Tyson's private life be a liability for Mu Theta?"

Looking at Kendrick, I can tell he is just as dumbfounded as I am about Arlen's remarks. It's like Arlen sipped from the proverbial Kool-Aid Lamont and Willie concocted. He managed to reiterate what those two had already argued, and yet put a sophisticated spin on it. I'm now feeling less confident about the potential for productivity of tonight.

"Okay, are you done?" Gavin grumbles.

"Yeah, I'm finished," Arlen replies.

"I just wanted to make sure you were done before I call you on your bullshit," Gavin scoffs. "You're right that our fraternity has a reputation for throwing the hottest parties and what not. And you're also right that who someone is sleeping with is none of the chapter's business. But everything you said after that is ridiculous. If you're going to say sexual practices can be used as criteria for rejecting someone's request for membership, then some people shouldn't have been let in this fraternity."

"What are you getting at," Arlen aggressively counters.

"While I'm not questioning anyone's sexuality, I will say that a few guys I knew before they became brothers had a reputation of being man whores," Gavin goes on to say. "They slept with anything with a vagina. However, these guys were welcomed with open arms into the fraternity because they brought a lot of positive things to the table, and were committed to the success of Beta Kappa Nu. I find trying to block Tyson from becoming a Beta to be a little hypocritical and immature. Willie and Lamont, I got love for you both, but you two got some growing up to do."

Thankfully there's an old head with some sense in the room. I appreciate that Gavin has an open mind, and appears not to be a homophobe. Lamont and Willie on the other hand, seem pissed, and Arlen offended. I'm surprised Arlen has not attempted to issue a rebuttal.

"Man," Lamont yells out. "I'm not trying to hear that shit. Marcus, what do you think?" Lamont completely dismisses Gavin's thoughts.

"Try to keep it cool and respectful Lamont," Marcus cautions. "We don't want more tension than there already is."

"Okay Marcus, my b," Lamont begrudgingly apologizes.

"In terms of my thoughts, I'll attempt to be brief," Marcus continues. "I don't know this Tyson kid personally, and whether he is gay or not doesn't matter to me. What does matter to me, is that one person who isn't even a Beta is causing this much friction in the chapter. I understand that you all voted fairly, and that those that want Tyson on this new line won a majority of the vote; but, I would advise the chapter to look again at the impact of this decision. If two members of the chapter feel that strongly about not wanting him to be a Beta at this point in time, then maybe you all can discuss delaying his pledge process. I want to make it clear that I'm not saying you all should never allow him in the fraternity. However, I think that you all should take a vote on postponing Tyson's opportunity for membership to a future semester. This could allow those that don't like Tyson more time to get to know him and warm up to him. All I want is for you guys not to damage the current brotherhood trying to add new brothers to the fold."

"That sounds reasonable to me," Willie claims. "Let me have some more time to get to know ole boy. If he truly wants to be a Beta, then he can wait a semester or two." Of course Willie would love this idea. The suggestion Marcus gave is essentially to take Tyson off this current line of pledges, which is what Willie wants. This *kick the can* solution would mean we as a chapter would wave the ever elusive *someday* card in Tyson's face. And I sense someday would never come for him should we decide in favor of this option.

"Uh…" Kendrick groans. "You want us to give into this temper tantrum? I mean Marcus, you have kids. If one of them threw a temper tantrum about a decision the family makes, would you cave in and not go forward with the family plan?" It's an interesting question that Kendrick poses to Marcus. I just sit quiet, waiting on the answer.

"I understand your argument Ken," Marcus begins. "But the difference is, my children are children, and you all are grown men. My children know that at the end of the day, I have the final decision regardless of how they feel. And while my children can't get up and leave my family because they are unhappy about a choice made, you all as grown men can completely walk away from being active in this brotherhood if you feel unhappy. I've witnessed brothers disown the organization because of big chapter blow ups, and I don't want that to happen with you guys. You all are better than that."

I hate to admit that Marcus makes sense. Although I know allowing Tyson to continue on with the pledge process is the right thing to do morally, I don't want my current brothers to feel alienated. But, I don't want to give into Lamont and Willie's stubbornness either. By doing that now, we would be establishing a terrible precedent for our chapter. Leave it to Marcus to make me feel less secure about my original hardline stance on Tyson.

"If it's that deep, I'll change my damn vote," James blurts out. "I'm tired of talking about this issue, and want to go back to being that productive and drama-free chapter again." Lamont must feel the tides turning in his favor because he is starting to smirk.

"James are you serious?" Kendrick shouts, with a look of disappointment.

"Ken, if he wants to change his mind, then let him," Lamont interjects. "In fact, why don't we just take another vote?"

"There is no need to take another vote," Kendrick replies. "The issue has already been decided, and the boys we selected have already been told they will be pledging together. They've even started hanging out to get to know one another."

"So what?" Willie bluntly retorts. "We are in control of this process, not those boys."

"What about David?" Chance chimes in. "He's not even here to vote."

"I'll call him," Lamont responds. "He can take a break from studying to say how he feels real quick. I'll put him on speakerphone so you all can hear his opinion." I can tell that this is about to get interesting.

"Okay, if we take another vote and Tyson doesn't make the cut, what do we tell him?" Chance cynically questions. "Sorry, but after further consideration we can't offer you membership after all. We think you're just too gay for us."

"We'll tell him that after further consideration, we think he should wait to join because he is just a freshman," Willie fires back. "Not many brothers came through this chapter as a freshman anyway, so it makes sense to tell him to that."

"I think you all really should just take another vote," Marcus intervenes. "And regardless of the outcome this time, everyone needs to be willing to put personal feelings aside and commit to moving forward as a chapter." Kendrick shoots Marcus a look that screams "butt out!"

"Fine, let's get this over with if we are going to do it," Kendrick grumbles. "We will do this vote by a simple show of hands. All those in favor of Tyson joining Beta Kappa Nu now, raise your hand." Kendrick and Chance quickly throw up their hands. I gradually lift my hand as well, despite having some reservations due to Marcus' expressed sentiments. James didn't side with us this time, which we already knew would be the case.

"Three in favor," Kendrick continues. "All those not in favor, raise your hand." Lamont, Willie, James, and Randy all signal their opposition. As it stands now, things aren't looking so good for the young freshman's fate in Beta.

"Let me go ahead and call David," Lamont states with a dubious grin. It's as if he knows without a doubt he has won this battle. I wonder if what's happening now has actually been orchestrated by Lamont and Willie in an effort to get their way. I mean had they gotten Marcus to back them, and then had Marcus persuade us to take another vote on Tyson. Furthermore, I'm starting to believe Lamont already convinced David to change his stance. I don't want to think Marcus or David are participating in such a scheme, but something feels a little suspicious about all of this.

"Yo David," Lamont says. "I know you're studying, but the frat needs your input on something real quick. We're taking another vote on Tyson. Right now, Willie, Randy, James, and I voted against the dude. Chance, Tristan, and Kendrick voted the same as last time. Are you trying to change your mind?"

"Why do we have to do this for a second time?" David asks. "And why right now? I still have a lot to review for this test tomorrow."

"It will only take a second," Lamont responds. "Either you want Tyson to be a Beta or you don't. That simple."

"Fine," David barks. "You said that you, Willie, Randy, and James voted against him. Why did James change his mind?"

"Hey David, it's me James. Man, I changed my mind because I'm tired of all the unnecessary drama. To me, it's not worth taking on the kid right now if he is causing this much tension."

"But you didn't change your mind because Tyson did something wrong?" David requests to know.

"Naw, he didn't do anything," James answers. There's now an awkward silence.

"David, you still there," Willie yells out.

"Yeah, I'm here. I was just thinking. So I think the chapter should…" Once David reveals his decision, the basement immediately starts to thin out as those unhappy with the final results of the vote quickly proceed to exit. Truth be told, even those happy by the results seem to be fleeing Marcus' home. Trying to follow the rest of the crowd out the door, I get up and walk over to the three big brothers in the room to say my goodbyes.

"I'll see you guys later," I tell them. "Thanks again for the advice. And thanks again Marcus for the pizza."

"Tristan before you go, let me holla at you," Marcus insists. I'm not sure why he wants to hold me back to talk and nobody else, but I'll oblige him. "If you really want to thank me, make sure that this chapter doesn't fall apart. Mu Theta just returned to Hamilton less than two years ago." Marcus is right. The chapter hasn't been back at Hamilton that long, and for it to fall apart due to some dumb internal conflict is crazy.

"I'll do my best," I promise.

"That's all I ask young blood," Marcus sighs.

March 7, 2009 (Saturday)

    Today marks one of the most important and joyous occasions of my life. It is officially my 21st birthday. I am now a real adult, and it feels great. Although technically one is seen as an adult in the U.S. at the age of eighteen, it is at age twenty-one where one really feels like a grown up. Although at eighteen I could vote, register for the draft, and do things without parental consent. Now I can get into any club I want, purchase my own liquor or wine, and even visit a casino. I'm no longer constricted by my age, so I can do anything that I want.

    Despite the fact I'm not an avid drinker, and the one and only time I've drank alcohol was last semester, I'm kind of eager to participate in the American tradition of being "carded" to purchase a bottle. Denise and Kendrick are actually on their way to my place to come pick me up and take me the liquor store by campus. This would be the second planned event for my birthday festivities. The first event was the annual celebratory birthday lunch with my mom that I went to earlier in the day. Even at age twenty-one, I still like spending time with my mom on or around my birthday. Heck she birthed me.

    "I gotta feeling, that tonight's gonna be a good night. That tonight's gonna be a good night. That tonight's gonna be a good, good night."

    I love my new ringtone. I changed it this morning to the Black Eye'd Peas "I Gotta Feeling" song, thinking it would be appropriate for my birthday. After the ringtone plays through once, I grab my phone to answer it.

    "Hey Ken."

"Hey T! Denise and I are downstairs in front of your building waiting on you. You ready to get your birthday drank?"

"Absolutely Ken! On my way down now." I grab my wallet and keys, and leave out the door.

****

Entering the liquor store, I find myself slightly overwhelmed by the vast selection of products. There are so many shelves and so many bottles to choose from in here. I'm glad Kendrick is here to offer his alcohol expertise.

"Ken, I have no idea what to get," I tell him, looking like a deer in headlights.

"Well let's try not to get anything that will have you too wasted," he suggests. "However, I want you to at least feel something on your birthday. How about some type of vodka?"

"Yeah Tristan, you may want to get vodka," Denise concurs. "Remember, I decided to get a certain brown liquor for my birthday, and after drinking it I couldn't remember anything besides the toilet bowl I was hunched over the next morning. Since you're not a heavy drinker, I recommend you stay away from the hard stuff." It's funny that my faux sister serves as a cautionary tale for this evening.

"I hear y'all," I reply. Continuing to walk past product after product, I stumble across a bottle of Cîroc. I had seen Diddy advertise it on television, and he made it seem like it's the best product ever. Plus, it is indeed a brand of vodka like Kendrick and Denise recommended. I think this will definitely be my drink of choice for the night. I grab some Cîroc and walk up to the register.

"Good choice T," Kendrick says. "You're prolly gonna like that."

"How you doin sugar?" the cashier asks. She's a middle aged white woman that smells like the world's first ashtray. However, she appears to be a nice person. "Do you have your I.D. on you handsome?" I gladly reach in my wallet, pull out my driver's license, and hand her the I.D.

"Here you go ma'am?" I proudly state.

"It's your birthday today I see," she giggles. "And you're 21st at that. Well happy birthday to ya."

"Thank you," I respond. "It feels great to finally be of age."

"I bet it does honey. I remember my twenty-first. My gal pals and I tore up the streets of D.C. Just my friends, some gin, and a few good men, partying it up in the city." I can tell that the cashier is starting to reminisce on her younger days.

"So when was that, two years ago," I joke. It's obvious that it's been sometime since she was in her twenties, but there's nothing wrong with being nice.

"Well aren't you just as sweet as you are handsome," she compliments. "You know what? I want you to take this as a little birthday gift. But don't you tell anyone you got this from me." She pulls a set of four shot glasses out, and places them in the black bag with my Cîroc.

"Oh wow, thank you very much," I exclaim. I then give her cash for the liquor, and she gives me my change.

"You make sure you and your friends have a great time tonight," she recommends. "And you be sure to find some girl to treat you nice if you catch my drift." I can't help but laugh at her well wishes.

"Ha, thanks," I chuckle. "And I have a special someone in mind that I hope will treat me right tonight." Kendrick, Denise, and I then make our way out of the store.

"Tristan, who is the special someone you were talking about?" Denise inquires.

"Oh, I'll let you know at some point," I answer. Tonight is definitely not the night I'm going to give her an unveiled look into my personal life.

"Kendrick do you know who this boy is talking about, since he won't tell me," Denise probes. "A boy turns twenty-one, and acts brand new." She is giving me a side eye accompanied with a smirk.

"Yeah I do," Kendrick grins. "But I only know because I caught Tristan with the special someone." It's cute seeing him play coy.

"So who is it," Denise demands to know.

"He will tell you when he gets ready Denise."

"Forget both of y'all then," she laughs. "I'm gonna find out who this mystery girl is! Mark my words!"

****

Having spent some time with my mom, and then purchasing my birthday bottle of alcohol, I now am getting ready for phase three of my birthday celebration. A night out partying at Club Fever. Club Fever is a new club on D.C.'s Waterfront for people twenty-one years of age and older. I've heard from several people on campus that this place is definitely the new hot spot in the city, so I thought it would be the perfect location to celebrate my grown status.

Pulling the clothes that I bought for tonight out of my Macy's shopping bag, my mind is riddled with thoughts about the potential awkwardness of tonight's festivities. I invited the entire Mu Theta chapter of Beta Kappa Nu to join me. After the outcome of the second vote on Tyson, Lamont and Willie again distanced themselves from the rest of us, claiming they didn't want to be a part of the "gay shit." Although I have been in contact with Lamont and Willie, Kendrick hadn't seen or heard from them since that night. He's still quite pissed at their ignorance, and they are still upset about his overwhelming support of Tyson. So, witnessing the interaction between the three is going to be interesting should Lamont and Willie show up at Club Fever.

Tonight also stands to be awkward because my friends from back home won't be able to celebrate with me. They are all under age, and don't have a good fake I.D. It feels odd not bringing in the big two one without my friends who I've known practically my whole life. However, we all planned to do it big for all of our 21st birthdays in July when the youngest of our bunch, Alex, finally becomes of age. My actual birthday is today though, so it's time to get in more of a party mindset, and to let my worries of the evening go.

As I get ready to hop into the shower, I hear someone knocking on my door. Once again my roommate Carter is not in the apartment to answer it. He isn't twenty-one yet either, and he couldn't come out with me to the city. Not one to stay in on a Saturday night though, he and some of his friends went to a house party out by the University of Maryland.

"Just a minute," I holler from the bathroom, pulling my pants back up and throwing my shirt back on so I don't answer the door nude. Finally getting to the door, I answer it and see Kendrick. "Oh…Hey Ken. I thought you were coming back to pick me up at 10:30." Last time I checked, the clock in my bedroom only read 9:50pm.

"I know that's what I said T, but I wanted to come over a little earlier and give you your birthday gift." He walks in my apartment with his hands behind his back, and I shut the door.

"You didn't have to get me anything," I state. "Being my driver for the night is already good enough."

"Of course I didn't have to get you anything T. All I have to do is stay black and die. I just wanted to give you something though because it's your special day, and you're special to me. So here you go. Happy Birthday!" From behind his back, Kendrick presents me with a red box. The kind of red box one would usually find a necklace of some sort in. I take the top off of the box and see two tickets. Upon closer inspection, I realize they are two tickets to see Beyoncé's *I Am…World Tour* in D.C.

"Ken what are these? Are you serious? How in the…?" I'm so excited and in awe right now, that it's becoming hard for me to keep it together.

"Ha, it's your birthday gift T, and I am very serious. Don't worry about the how. Just know that you have two tickets to see your favorite artist. Well, one ticket. I was hoping you would ask me to go with you."

"Of course I want you to go with me. But these are great seats, so I know these tickets must have cost you a grip. I can't accept these." Though it pains me to say this, I just don't think I could take such an expensive gift.

"Tristan Steele, you are taking these tickets and that's that! If it makes you feel any better, I got a great deal on them." Since he called me by my first and last name, I know he's getting a little annoyed with my apprehension.

"Nothing left to say then I guess but thank you," I exclaim. "You're absolutely amazing, you know that?" I give him a quick hug and kiss on the lips. "You're the best boyfriend ever!" Oh no! I can't believe I dropped the B word. We've never called each other that before. Maybe somehow he didn't hear me.

"Did you just call me your boyfriend?" he questions. Well it's clear that he heard me.

"Um, let's chalk that little slip of the tongue to my excitement," I try to laugh off.

"Oh, well too bad," Kendrick responds. "I kind of like the sound of that boyfriend thing."

"Really Ken?"

"Yeah T! We've been friends going on two years, and have been basically dating for a few months now. Why wouldn't I like the sound of you calling me your boyfriend?" He has a point. Maybe calling him my boyfriend is not such a crazy idea, but we just haven't had a conversation about the label yet. And I didn't expect to have it on my birthday.

"What are you saying then?" I ask.

"I'm saying I don't mind you calling me your boyfriend," he replies.

"I actually don't mind if you call me your boyfriend either," I shyly mutter.

"Then I guess we are boyfriends then," Kendrick laughs.

"I guess so." I again start kissing my now boyfriend. It's crazy that I entered my first real relationship so haphazardly.

"Since we are now officially boo'd up T, you wanna go back to your room and celebrate for real?"

"We are supposed to pick up Denise in about thirty minutes or so, and I've still got to shower and get dressed," I tell him.

"T, I'll just tell Denise that I'm running late, and I'll be by to scoop her in about an hour."

"In that case, let's celebrate!"

****

"The line to get in this place is ridiculous," Denise claims as her, Kendrick, Rob, and I stand in line to get into Club Fever. I told Denise to invite Rob out to join us. They have been dating casually since they met at the inaugural ball.

"Yeah it is," I cosign. "Good thing we took a few shots of that Cîroc before we left campus to keep us warm while we wait out here." After I finally got dressed, Kendrick and I headed to Denise's apartment in the building next to mine. I took the bottle I had bought earlier along with the gifted shot glasses to her apartment, and there Denise and I knocked back several shots. Kendrick opted not to join us in taking any shots because he's our driver for the night.

"Hey, we don't have to wait in this line," Rob points out. "The short guy working the front door is actually one of my friends from back home. I'm sure he will let us in with no problems. We probably have to pay the cover though." Not wanting to spend thirty or forty minutes outside in the cold waiting to get in this place, I'm glad to hear about Rob's connect.

"Well lead the way," I blurt out. The four of us bypass the rest of the people standing in line, and go up to Rob's friend.

"Gerard, what's going on?" Rob greets the short guy.

"Hey Big Rob," Gerard hollers. "Man what's up? How have you been? I haven't seen you since Jasmine's birthday party."

"I've been good," Rob answers. "Just been doing the school thing. You and your girl still together?"

"Of course we are Rob. You know she can't quit me. We are actually having a kid in a few months."

"Man that's great Gerard. Congrats!"

"Appreciate that," Gerard says. "Excited to see my seed. You feel me? But yo, you trying to get in here tonight?"

"Sure am. Actually me and my three friends here."

"Alright cool," Gerard replies. "Let me just see everyone's I.D." We each give him our license, and he checks the date of birth on each one. "Oh it's your birthday." Gerard is now looking at me. "You go ahead and go in, don't worry about paying a cover. Unfortunately the rest of you have to pay twenty bucks."

"Thanks for that," I tell him.

"No problem," Gerard states. "You all have a great time inside. And Rob, I'll hit you up later." Denise, Kendrick, and Rob hand their money to Gerard, and after being padded down by a large gentleman, we all walk into the venue.

"It's real live in here," I yell. I'm trying to talk over the loud music. I really am fascinated by all I see in here so far.

To my left is the bar that is bombarded with patrons trying to buy a drink. On my right is the coat check line. I guess the four of us were all thinking alike, because none of us brought a coat to check. That's an extra club expense no one wanted to incur. Walking deeper into this place, I notice a variation of black guys wearing the standard club uniform, jeans and a buttoned down shirt. Standing around the guys, or in some cases bent over in front of them, are women dressed in their "freakum dress" and highest heels.

"Tristan, what do you think?" Denise questions.

"It's cool," I answer.

"Okay, well let's go get you a birthday drink on me," she insists. I'm already a little buzzed. Those shots I had are starting to hit me. However, I'm not going to decline her offer.

"Thanks Denise," I chuckle. Following her to the bar, my eyes land on Lamont, Willie, James, and David.

"Hey what's up fellas," I say.

"Tristan," David exclaims. "Happy birthday! You're finally grown!"

"My line brother is finally legal," Lamont adds. "I'm going to make sure your ass gets drunk tonight!"

"I don't know about all of that," I mumble. My party guests and I again start walking toward the bar.

****

I have not the slightest clue as to what time it is, or how long I've been on this dance floor dancing. What I do know is that I have surpassed the point of being buzzed or tipsy. I am pretty certain that I'm drunk. Although I'm not stumbling or drastically slurring my words, I can't feel my face, it's becoming harder to visually focus, and I can't stop dancing. I've done everything from a simple two step, to the "Stanky Leg," to the "Dougie." To my brothers, Denise, and Rob, I'm the life of the party. They all are having as much fun as I am.

Kendrick on the other hand, is trying to enjoy himself; however, he appears to be too concerned about me or just ready to go home. Or perhaps both. I can't blame him for wanting to leave though. He's sober in a sea of intoxicated people. Additionally, things between Lamont, Willie, and Kendrick haven't been going that well. Even though the two factions haven't really spoken all night, the tension is so thick, I think if anyone of them says more than a hello or a goodbye to each other, a brawl will breakout.

"Yo Tristan," Lamont shouts, grabbing my arm. "This right here is Christina." Emerges from behind him is this beautiful brown skin girl. She's quite short and petite, with the biggest breasts I've ever seen.

"How you doing?" she asks me. I'm a little confused as to what's going on here.

"I'm great," I begin. "And you, Christina?"

"Hey," Lamont interrupts. "I told Christina here that it's your birthday, and she said she had to meet you and show you some love."

"Oh I appreciate that," I thank her. Even drunk, I know how weird this whole exchange is.

"I haven't shown you any birthday love yet cutie," she snickers seductively. Then the DJ cues T-Pain's "Can't Believe It" out of nowhere. Christina practically throws me up against the wall and commences grinding on me in between my legs. Feeling like I'm on display in front of my brothers and Denise,

I dance in tune with Christina's hips to put on a show. While working to impress my dance partner and audience, I glance over at Kendrick and try to focus my eyesight. I want to see if he looks bothered by the way I'm dancing. I don't know if such intimate contact with a girl is in violation of our newly defined relationship. From what I can tell, Kendrick has his arms folded; and yet, his face is displaying his award-winning smile.

"You like that baby?" Christina asks. She then turns around to face me, and attempts to place her lips on mine. I'm able to dodge her attempt to kiss me by jerking my head back. I again look at Kendrick and notice that his smile has disappeared. His jaw is tightening and that vein above his eyebrow is forming. He is actually approaching me.

"Tristan, you about ready to get out of here?" Kendrick questions, towering over me and my dance partner.

"Fall back," Lamont tells Kendrick with more base in his voice than necessary. "Can't you see Tristan is getting him some action? I mean damn, you blocking." I'm now sobering up rather quickly, because I'm fearful that a confrontation may be in the very near future. I nudge Christina to excuse herself from our group.

"I'm talking to Tristan," Kendrick counters with his chest slightly puffed up. "I'm getting a headache and we've been here for about three hours." Lamont now takes a slight step toward Kendrick, and Willie steps up behind Lamont.

"Why don't you just go home then, and we'll bring him back with us," Willie chimes in. "No need to drag him up out of here just because you're ready to leave."

"As soon as Tristan tells me he's not ready to go and wants to stay, then I'll be out of here," Kendrick claps back. I think it's best that I go with Kendrick. The situation with

Christina I know made him feel some type of way, and I'm not a fan of Lamont and Willie teaming up against him. Besides, after apparently three hours of dancing, I'm tired anyway.

"That's alright Willie," I interject. "I'm ready to get out of here actually. It's been a great birthday, but I'm beat."

"Man, that's some bullshit, but alright Tristan," Willie yields.

Lamont then for some reason again directs his attention to Kendrick. "I swear you're a hatin' ass nigga sometimes. Just because you're not having a good time and not getting any play but Tristan is, you want to leave all of a sudden and take him with you." I'm thankful Christina had taken the hint to leave, and Denise and Rob, although spectators of this chapter beef, are not close enough to hear what's being said.

"Whoa Lamont, chill," David interrupts, stepping in front of Lamont. "It's not that deep."

"Naw David," Lamont continues. "He is ruining Tristan's birthday because he's jealous. And shit, maybe he's not jealous about not getting any play. Maybe he's upset because ole girl got to dance with Tristan and he didn't. Kendrick didn't start getting a headache until Christina came over here. Is that it Kendrick? You mad you can't have Tristan? I've been telling y'all this nigga is gay ever since that Tyson situation came up." I'm completely sober at this point, and it didn't take water or food to get me here.

"For real Lamont, you need to chill out," I demand. "I can't believe you're gonna do this to your own line brother. Especially here, and on my birthday. That's foul and you know it." Although I want to dropkick Lamont in his Adam's apple for trying to embarrass Kendrick, I find some inner peace and hold on to it.

"Yo forget you Lamont," Kendrick hollers. "I'm not about to defend myself to your ignorant ass. I'm getting out of here." Kendrick then storms off. I start to walk behind Kendrick toward the exit. Since Denise and Rob were watching the whole incident unfold and could see Kendrick and me leaving, they too make their way to the door.

"Ken, wait up," I call out as I try to keep up with him. He continues to walk fast though until he is on the outside of Club Fever. Once I finally catch up with him, we stand in silence waiting on Denise and Rob.

"Is everything okay?" Denise questions as she and Rob approach us. "I saw you guys get into it. I assume it was a fraternity thing."

"Um, we're fine," Kendrick mumbles. "We're just ready to head out of here. You ready to go?"

"Oh yeah sure," she tells us. "I'm going to walk with Rob to his car, and have him drive me over to where you parked. If that's okay?"

"Denise, I can just take you back to campus," Rob offers. "I don't mind. Besides, I wanted to see if you wanted to go and get some breakfast."

"Well in that case, I'll see you guys back on campus," Denise says to me and Kendrick.

"Text me when you get back," I request.

"Will do," she agrees.

"Nice to meet you Kendrick," Rob states, preparing to head to his car. "And happy birthday again Tristan."

"Thanks," I respond. As Denise and Rob leave, Kendrick and I walk to the parking lot to get in Kendrick's SUV.

"I can't believe I call those assholes my brothers," Kendrick angrily grunts. "Thankfully in a few months when I graduate, I won't have to deal with them anymore."

"I'm sorry that all of that went down in there," I apologize. "I'm just as blown as you are. I never expected things between you and Lamont and Willie to escalate like that. I'm also sorry about that whole Christina thing. I didn't mean to upset you by dancing with her. And you saw I pulled away from her when she tried to kiss me."

"T, there is no need for you to apologize for their dumbass behavior. You didn't tell them to blatantly disrespect me. As far as the whole Christina thing, I'm not mad y'all were dancing. It did bother me that she tried to kiss you though. In that moment, I felt she was getting a little too close."

"Ken, no matter how close she got, or how close anyone gets to me, know that you don't have to worry about anything happening. You're my boo thang. I'll duck and dodge as many people as I need to in order to protect what we have. Heck, you've seen my dance moves, I'm more than capable." His vein starts to disappear again, and he hints at a smile.

"Ha, thanks T. Sorry for ruining your birthday." We arrive at Kendrick's whip and climb in.

"Are you kidding me," I gasp. "Because of you, this has been one of the most memorable birthdays ever. So thank you."

"You're welcome," Ken whispers.

March 18, 2009 (Wednesday)

"I can't believe it's this time of year again," I tell David, Chance, and Kendrick. We are all in one of the on-campus dance studios, preparing to have our first official practice for Hamilton's annual Greek step show.

"Well believe it," David exclaims. "We've only got six weeks to put together a winning show, so we have to get to work." Since David has become the captain of the step team, he has taken his position quite seriously. Prior to today, he sent out a mass text letting the whole chapter know that if any of us wants to step in the competition, that we have to show up to every mandatory practice from now until the actual day of the event. If any of us miss a practice, then we would run the risk of him cutting us from the team. I could tell by the message that he meant business, so here I am, along with Chance. Although Kendrick is not planning to step, he's here because he's great at taking care of show logistics. He's going to work with David in coordinating future practice times, and ensuring we as a team have everything we need in order to carry out David's vision.

"Alright I hear you David," I chuckle. "Well is it just me, you, and Chance stepping? I mean, where are James and Randy?" I don't even bother asking about Lamont and Willie, because they both are still claiming to be done with fraternity business.

"They should be walking through the door any minute now," David answers. "As soon as they get here we can get started."

"Okay cool," I say. "And what time are we supposed to meet up with these new boys tonight again?" Even with all the chapter drama, Mu Theta as a whole is still committed to bringing in Tyson and the rest of his line brothers. The boys have been pledging Beta Kappa Nu now for several weeks, and are close to being a legitimate part of our brotherhood.

"I told them we would meet up with them at 10:30, which is why I told y'all to meet here at the studio at 8:30 so we can get about two hours of practice in beforehand," David scoffs in slight frustration. The clock on the wall reads 8:40. "Randy and James need to hurry up and get here." The door opens.

"Chill, we're here," Randy announces as him and James saunter through the studio doors.

"My bad we're late," James apologizes. "We were driving back onto campus, and the Hamilton police pulled me over for a broken tail light."

"Yeah they got him for a DWW," Randy jokes.

"A what?" Chance inquires.

"You know, a DWW," Randy repeats. "Instead of pulling him over for driving while black, they pulled him over for driving while white." Unfortunately for Randy, it seems his joke fell flat.

"Whatever Randy," Chance chuckles.

"Sorry to hear that James," David says. "Well let's go ahead and get practice started. It will help get your mind off of things."

****

"Why in the hell did I agree to step," James huffs. We are all a little winded after nearly two hours of step practice.

"Because you want to rep for Beta, and help bring home that trophy again," David grins.

"Ugh, I guess," James struggles to get out. "At least we're done for the night. Right?"

"Yeah we're done," David says.

"Alright bet," James sighs with relief. "Well I guess it's time to go meet up with the new guys. I'm gonna swing by the store real quick and catch up with you guys. I got to get some Gatorade or something."

"Wait up James, I'm gonna ride with you," Randy claims. As the both of them begin to walk to the exit, the door opens.

"Yo, what's good," Willie greets with Lamont right behind him. Since this practice is technically Beta related business, I'm surprised to see them come through the door. And judging by Kendrick's facial expression, so is he.

"Hey," David starts. "We're just finishing practice. You all should have been here at 8:30 if you wanted to step in the show."

"Ha, chill," Lamont snickers. "We aren't trying to be on the step team. Chance told us to come by around this time because he said he had something important to tell us in person. Something that couldn't wait."

"Yeah, I told them to come by," Chance interjects. "I have something to share with all of you really." Randy and James back away from the door, Lamont and Willie find spots on the wall to lean on, and Kendrick, David, and I stop moving to pay attention. Ironically, the tension that exists between Kendrick, Lamont, and Willie has vanished in the moment. I think we are all just concerned by what's so important that Chance has to tell us.

"Look," Chance continues. "I'll cut to the chase. I couldn't make it to Tristan's birthday thing last weekend, but I heard what happened. All this stuff has to stop. The back and forth between you guys, between you brothers, has gone too far. Lamont and Willie, you have to let go of this new aged witch hunt y'all got going on, trying to figure out who's gay and who's not. It's costing you a brotherhood and friendship." With insight on what Chance wants to discuss, the tension within the chapter immediately resurfaces.

"Chance, you can't tell me you don't think Tyson and this nigga Kendrick are gay," Willie bellows.

"Willie you're missing the point," Chance goes on to say. "Whether they are gay or not shouldn't affect you or impact your involvement in Beta Kappa Nu. When you pledged to be a Beta and a part of this chapter, you did so knowing this is an organization with all kinds of men. Black and white, short and tall, Christian and Muslim. And believe it or not, there are both heterosexual and homosexual Betas too. Regardless of color, religion, and sexuality, at the end of the day, all these men are your brothers. All these brothers vowed to have your back, and it's messed up that you and Lamont are acting like your brotherhood is conditional."

With the room quiet and motionless, Chance directs his full attention to Lamont. "I think I'm more surprised by you. Kendrick is your line brother, and you've basically turned on him. You two pledged together. This is the same line brother that loaned you $500 to get your car out of the impound lot a few months ago. In fact, he's the same one that took you to the airport at four in the morning last Christmas Eve. Now that you all don't agree on something and you suspect he's gay, you negate all you two have been through and what he's done for you? And you don't even know if he's gay. You're just accusing him with no proof." I'm appreciative of Chance's candor right now. I only wish he dropped this knowledge sooner.

"Chance, I get everything you're saying," Lamont responds. "And Kendrick has held me down in the past." Is Lamont finally about to take a step in the right direction? "But I can't have people thinking I'm gay, or support this gay shit." I guess not. "As long as you all continue to pledge Tyson, and niggas like him, I can't rock with this chapter. I'll still talk to certain brothers outside of fraternity business, but anything to do with Beta the fraternity at Hamilton, I won't be around. There may be homos that are Betas, but I don't rock with any. And I don't want to."

"Now Kendrick," Lamont redirects, looking directly at my boyfriend. "As my line brother, I should have given you the benefit of the doubt about being gay. So, if you tell me right here and right now that you're straight and only like females, then I will apologize for calling you out and I'll never do it again." Everyone's mouth is open, but no one seems to be able to speak. I think we're all eagerly waiting on Kendrick's response. Even I am on pins and needles. I may know the truth about Kendrick, but I'm not sure if he will allow Lamont to pressure him into sharing it in this moment.

"First off, let me say this," Kendrick begins. "I think it's real foul you won't give me an apology regardless for the way you tried to put me on blast at Club Fever. That was plain disrespectful. And believe me, the only reason you didn't get swung on was because I didn't want to ruin Tristan's birthday, and I know how bad it would have looked for two Betas to be in a fight in public."

"Forget that," Willie interrupts. "Do you like men or women? Yes or no? Damn!"

"Whoa Willie," David adds. "You got to let the man talk. Calm down!"

"Don't worry about it David," Kendrick counters. "I got this. Since Lamont and Willie seem to be so pressed to know, I'll tell you all; although, it's not anyone's business. I do in fact prefer men. So yes, I'm a black gay man." I can't believe he just came out. Knowing that he transferred into Hamilton because he was treated so poorly at his other school once people found out that he's gay, I'm surprised he just made this revelation. However, I'm proud and impressed by his courage in this moment.

"I knew it," Lamont exclaims. "About damn time, shit! I've been telling y'all this nigga was gay."

"Right," Willie seconds. "He's been lying to us this whole time."

"I haven't lied to y'all," Kendrick quickly quips. "I didn't pretend to be anything. I never claimed to like girls, and I never denied that I like men. But now that it's out there, what do you expect to happen? Do you think I'm going to suddenly disappear? I'm not going to stop being a Beta, and I for damn sure am not going to let you, Lamont, or anybody else with immature insecurities shame me into my apartment until I graduate!" This conversation is starting to resemble a tennis match at Wimbledon. Kendrick just hit an incredible serve to Lamont and Willie, and the rest of us in the room watch closely to see if these two could return it.

"Okay, so now Kendrick himself said he is gay," Lamont shouts. "No one besides me and Willie have a problem with it? Y'all act like this shit doesn't matter, but it does. When people on campus find out he's a fag, they are going to think we all take it in the ass." With this inflammatory comment Lamont just spouted, I would say he just returned Kendrick's so called "serve" with a vengeance, but it was way out of bounds.

"Lamont, I let you slide so far with all the insults and ignorant comments, but you better not call me that word again," Kendrick warns. I'm now able to tell with certainty that he's pissed, because the infamous vein reappears.

"Let me," Lamont rhetorically asks. "I'm a grown man, so you don't let me do anything. I'm going to say what I want, and no bitch ass punk is going to check me. Faggot!" I'm not sure if I have a vein of my own or not, but I'm livid. Not only am I highly offended by the incendiary word Lamont insists on dropping, but I'm beyond tired of him routinely disrespecting someone so important to me. I've had about enough.

"Yo," Kendrick shoots back as he quickly stands up and approaches Lamont. "Why don't you suck this faggot's dick you dumbass fuck." Kendrick is now grabbing himself. I'm taken aback by his retort. He's usually not the type to say something like this; but, I usually don't see him this angry. I guess people can say almost anything once they've reached their boiling point.

"You'd like that wouldn't you," Lamont jabs while trying to stand as tall as he possibly could in front of Kendrick, who's about a head taller. "Man, back your gay ass out of my face." Lamont shoves Kendrick, knocking him back a few inches. With this initiation of contact, a switch flips on inside of me. My heart is beating uncontrollably fast, and my breathing is becoming louder and louder. Now consumed by my own anger, I dart over to Kendrick's defense.

"What the hell is wrong with you?" I yell at Lamont. I'm now in between these two men with Kendrick behind me.

"With me?" Lamont questions. "He's the one that just came at me. And you better not stand in front of him like that, he might try to get you in the ass. Batty boy!" On instinct, I grab Lamont by the neck hole of his shirt, and throw him up against the wall.

"You say one more disrespectful thing to him, and I promise you Imma beat your ass," I threaten. I've never been in a real fight before, but I'm ready to change that if need be.

"Get your damn hands off me," Lamont commands. He's desperately trying to break free from my grasp, but is so far unsuccessful. The more he struggles, the tighter I press him against the wall. All of my brothers rush around us, and try to intervene. I can hear them around me, pleading for me to let go. Out of the corner of my left eye, I can see Willie attempting to lunge at me, but James and Chance somehow are able to hold back his football player build.

"Tristan stop," Kendrick requests. "It's not worth it!"

"No Ken," I reply. "He's got to learn a lesson. He can't keep treating you like this."

"Why the hell are you defending him?" Lamont demands to know. "Are you gay too?"

"Yeah asshole, I am gay, and Kendrick is my man. So the more you come at him, the more we are going to have a damn problem."

Oh gosh, what did I just do? Did I really just come out? And on top of that, did I voluntarily announce that I'm in a relationship with Kendrick? How could I let my anger get the best of me like this? Lord, please let this be a horrible nightmare, because I'm truly not ready for the fallout of my irrational behavior if this is real.

"You're what," Willie barks. "Oh hell naw!" With the first negative response to my sexuality, I let go of Lamont and back away from him and all my brothers. "I can't do this anymore, I'm out of here." Willie opens the door to the studio and storms out.

"Wait up Willie," Lamont calls out. "I'm rolling out of here too. I'm done with this chapter. Good luck with the homos fellas!" He then follows suit and leaves. It's now Chance, Randy, James, David, Kendrick, and I left in the room. With the exception of Kendrick, I feel everyone is gawking at me like I'm some science experiment they're viewing under a microscope. I'm not sure how to handle this predicament that I've gotten myself in. I've just got to go. If NASA were selling tickets, I'd be on the first thing to the moon. I grab my black drawstring backpack and bolt out the door.

"Tristan, hold up," Kendrick pleads, following out of the door behind me. "Where are you going? You want to talk about this?"

"Ken, I have to have some space. I'll hit you up later." I really want to be by myself to process the fact that I literally tore the door, along with the hinges, off my closet.

"Um okay T. Please call me later."

"Yeah sure," I mumble.

March 19, 2009 (Thursday)

Last night I think I slept a total of two hours. My mind could not shake everything that happened yesterday. I kept recapping every word said and every move made in that impromptu meeting. It was just supposed to be a regular step practice; but once Tweedledum and Tweedledee showed up, it turned into quite the disaster. I get that Chance invited these two in one last attempt to unite the chapter; however, his last ditch effort was an utter failure.

There was no hope of unification once Lamont went into one of his ignorant rants. How could anyone think we would again be this cohesive and happy chapter, with such stupidity present? I mean honestly.

Although the level of disrespect was outrageous last night, I wonder if I did the right thing by responding the way I did. Lamont and Willie kept hurling insults at Kendrick, trying to belittle him and nullify his manhood. What was I supposed to do as Kendrick's fraternity brother? More importantly, as his boyfriend? Those two idiots should be thankful I didn't throw punches. Of course at 6'8" I know Kendrick was more than capable of defending himself, but enough was enough. I had reached my boiling point. I couldn't hear another ugly insult.

And in the midst of everything going on yesterday, Kendrick boldly unveiled himself in a room full of our heterosexual fraternity brothers. Although he is not ashamed of who he is, he always desired to keep his private life private. I can't understand why he would let Lamont and Willie pressure him into disclosing his sexuality. After hours of foregoing sleep, the best theory I can come up with is that he in a way wanted to reclaim the power back from the homophobes. By basically saying "yes I'm gay, so what," Kendrick neutralized the two, and basically let them know that they will no longer use his identity as a weapon to harm him. Put in this perspective, it was extremely brave and clever.

The kicker of yesterday was that I allowed my anger in the situation lead me to confessing something I wasn't quite prepared for the world to hear. Unlike Kendrick, I didn't intentionally make my "I'm gay" declaration. I literally just came to accept my own sexuality. Heck, a few months ago I was on the brink of suicide due to my identity crisis. And although I'm confident in who I am, I'm not confident in how those closest to me will perceive this Tristan Steele.

Tired and stressed about the future status of my relationships, I want nothing more than to lie in this bed all day. Unfortunately, I have to be at work by 8:00am and it's already 7:30. I'm trying to find something to wear in my clothes hamper to iron quickly so I can get out of here. In the three years I've lived away from home, I've developed a bad habit of washing my clothes, and then just leaving them in the basket instead of putting them away. Searching for pants to put on, I hear my phone go off. Taking a peak, I see a message from Kendrick.

Kendrick: Hey Tristan. I hope everything is ok. I know you said you just needed some time to think, but I'm a little worried about you. Can you at least tell me if you're okay?

I feel a little bad for shutting Kendrick out, but I honestly didn't want to be comforted by him yesterday. Had I spoken to him last night, he would have tried to tell me everything will be alright. But the fact of the matter is, he doesn't know if everything will be alright. He doesn't know for certain how the revelation of my sexuality will impact my relationships with my mom and best friends. And I just didn't feel like being gassed with imaginative positivity last night.

Me: I'm fine. But I'm actually rushing to get ready for work, can I talk to you later?

Kendrick: Sure. You want to come by my place to chill tonight?

Me: Yeah. I'll be by when I get off work and out of my last class.

Kendrick: Ok bet. I'll see you then.

  I don't necessarily feel like being comforted today either, but I don't want Kendrick to feel like I was avoiding him. Isolating myself in the past offended Kendrick, and I rather not repeat that mistake again. But anyway, where are my damn dress pants? I've got to get to work.

****

  Thank God it's time for me to leave this office. If I didn't know any better, I would have thought I was trapped in a time warp, where minutes go by extremely slow. I barely did any actual work today. Between trying to stay awake and trying to keep my mind off my personal problems, I couldn't really focus. My student staff kept coming up to me, asking about their schedules and about issues they ran into with clients, and it was hard for me to even pretend to care.

  It's a shame that I have a class I have to go to before I can file this day away as over. Everything within me is telling me to skip class today, and head to my apartment. I have a good grade in the class, and I wouldn't be paying attention sitting in a classroom anyway. Plus, I've been trying to quasi duck and dodge Beta brothers around campus, fearful things are weird now. Walking across campus to go to class increases my likelihood of running into them. Thankfully, Chance no longer works in the office with me. It's decided. I'm going back to my apartment to lie down. I'll send a text to one of my classmates and ask her to let me know if I miss something important.

As the other student employees begin to vacate the office, I make one more final sweep to make sure the computers are shut down, the phones are forwarded, and the back door to the office is locked. Since everything checks out, it's time to go. I grab my backpack and head out the front door. Attempting to be incognito, I walk toward one of the side stairwells to get out of here relatively unnoticed by the masses.

"Hey Tristan, wait up," A voice calls out. I haven't even made it to the staircase yet before I'm spotted. What I wouldn't give to be invisible right now. Turning around I see Tyson. The usually well-dressed and well-groomed freshman stands before me in grey sweat pants, a black hoodie, and black moccasins. His beard and mustache can best be described as straggly, and his hairline is hidden somewhere underneath his uncut curly jet black hair.

"Tyson, what's up? And I hope you're not just hanging out in here." It's a rule in the fraternity that those pledging were not allowed to be hanging out and about around campus. The premise of the rule is that one shouldn't have time to hang out if he is adequately dividing his time between school, studying to be a Beta man, and other responsibilities he may have.

"Oh no sir," he replies. "I was actually trying to catch up with you before you left your office. You didn't show up last night with the older brothers for our session, so I just thought I'd check to see if you were okay."

"That wasn't necessary, but thanks," I tell him. "You know I've missed a session before?" Although I've made it a point to attend most of the new pledges' sessions, there were a few times I was absent due to more pressing obligations. So I'm not quite sure why he is making a big deal of this absence.

"Yes I know," he answers. "But I heard some of the big brothers talking yesterday. And…well…I thought I come check on you?" Dammit. I knew my chapter brothers were going to discuss what happened last night, but I didn't think they were going to talk about it in front of the new guys. I suddenly feel two feet tall.

"Really," I inquire, trying to play it cool. "What did they say that made you think I wasn't alright?"

"Well….um…," Tyson starts. "From what I heard, it sounds like you may have gotten into a fight with Lamont. And the fight was all because of me."

"Oh," I sigh. It kind of sounds like he knows bits and pieces of the story, but he doesn't know it all. "Even though I unfortunately got into a disagreement with my line brother, know that you weren't the real cause of it. What happened between us was bound to happen sooner or later."

"Look Tristan, you don't have to lie. I know that Lamont and Willie don't want me to be a Beta, and I know that it's because they think I'm gay." How in the heck did Tyson hear that information? He's either incredibly nosey, or my chapter brothers and I are terrible with discretion.

"I mean, that's why Lamont and Willie have never come around us pledges right? They don't support me? But you do. And that's the reason you fought last night. Since I was a kid, I've always wanted to be a brother of Beta Kappa Nu. I'd see my dad's nalia on the wall, and hear his stories, and knew I would one day pledge Beta. I just didn't imagine I'd destroy a chapter to do it. I've been thinking about quitting, so I don't cause any more problems with you guys."

This poor kid. He thinks I got into a fight because of him. While the start of Mu Theta's problems may have originated due to Willie and Lamont's strong opposition to Tyson's Beta membership, by no means was he the real cause of our issues. I can't blame him for their ignorance, and I definitely can't let him quit.

"Tyson, trust me, you aren't to blame for anything. Lamont and I fought because of him, and him alone. Not you. If you meant what you said about Beta, then you better not let the stuff going on with me and my line brother ever discourage you from pursuing it. Even if you don't ever click with Lamont or Willie, remember you have people in your corner, myself included. Now you get out of here and go to class or go study or something." Tyson is looking up at me smiling. I guess I alleviated whatever guilt or concern that he had.

"Sir," he chuckles. "Thanks for the pep talk. Please don't tell anyone I told you I thought about quitting."

"Your secret is safe with me," I promise. "I'll talk to you later."

"Okay Tristan. See you!" Tyson leaves and I again make my way to the stairwell, except I'm walking even faster. I don't want to be stopped again.

****

I'm so glad I skipped class to take that nap. As I approach the front door to Kendrick's apartment, I feel rested and of fresh mind. Which is a good thing, considering I'm at Kendrick's to discuss our joint exit out of the closet.

"Hey T, come on in," Kendrick welcomes me as I cross the threshold of his apartment. Closing the door behind me, he pulls me into a tight embrace.

"Hey Ken, how are you?" I ask, pulling back from him slightly so I can properly greet my boyfriend with a kiss.

"I'm alright," he answers after kissing me. We part and make our way to his sofa. "I should be asking you how you are. You had quite the day yesterday."

"Ha, well I guess we both did," I counter.

"So how do you feel T? Do you feel like a weight has been lifted a bit?"

"Um…Not exactly," I tell him. "I mean don't get me wrong, part of me does feel a little liberated. The fact that I don't have to hide my sexuality from our brothers anymore is a relief. But to be honest, I think I just bit off more than I can chew."

"I guess I understand," he mumbles, appearing slightly confused.

"Ken, I announced that I was a homosexual yesterday. And while part of me feels like this burden has been lifted or whatever, most of me is terrified. I envisioned me coming out to be different. I thought I would tell those closest to me one by one when I got ready. But now I feel because I haphazardly broadcasted my sexuality in the midst of my anger, that I've lost control of my narrative to those that matter to me the most. I no longer get to wait until I'm ready to tell my mom and best friends, but I'm rushed to tell them now. I can't afford those closest to me finding out this news from someone other than me."

"Okay I think I get it now," Kendrick nods. "Well who said you had to rush to do anything. Most of your best friends don't even attend Hamilton. Alex, Darius, and Isaac are all off at their own universities or doing their own thing, so no one from here will get the opportunity to tell them you're gay anytime soon. So you still have some time. As for Denise, you may want to tell her sooner rather than later because she is on campus. However, I think she will be fine once she hears the news. I can tell she seems ride or die for you T."

"True," I agree. "I guess I don't have to necessarily worry about Alex and the guys. But do you really think Denise won't freak out when she finds out I like men?" I want to believe Kendrick is right about her. I want to believe my collegiate sister will respond like he says she will.

"T, I'm about 95% sure. As far as your mom goes, I can't promise you how she will respond once she finds out. I will say that I think deep down, moms always know their sons. When I came out to my mom three years ago, she barely blinked an eye. She just wanted to know what took me so long to tell her. Now that she knows I'm gay, we are actually closer than ever, and talk about any and everything."

"Wow Ken, I wish. I can only hope my mom reacts like yours did. My gut tells me she won't be quite as accepting. But since she isn't at Hamilton, I guess I don't necessarily have to be in a big hurry to tell her I'm gay either."

"No you don't," he seconds. "I know it's hard for you to do, but try not to stress out about this. The people in your life that truly love you, won't care that you sleep with men. While some may not accept it right off the bat, those that love Tristan will accept you for you in due time." I have no idea how Kendrick always knows what to say, and when to say it.

His words of wisdom are just what I needed to hear to gain some perspective.

"Thanks," I tell him. "Has anyone ever told you that you have a gift for dropping some knowledge?"

"No, I don't believe anyone has told me that before," he replies. "And if you really want to thank me, you know you could…" Kendrick grins from ear to ear, while looking down at his lap.

"Ha….I could what," I tease. "Wash your pants?"

"You sure can wash them," he quips. "As soon as we're done."

"Done with what exactly," I joke.

"You'll soon find out," he snickers, before pulling me into a kiss.

"Wait," I interrupt, as I pull away from him. "I have one more thing to say."

"What is it," he asks.

"Before any laundry needs to be done, can I get a sandwich first? Haven't really stopped to eat all day."

"You're going to make me wait so you can eat some ham and turkey," Kendrick chuckles.

"Well yes," I laugh.

"You're cold blooded T. But let's go make you that sandwich." We start cracking up as we head to the kitchen.

It's amazing to think, that when I first came to Hamilton, it was all about me pursing my degree in criminology. However, I've unexpectedly learned more about myself than anything. It's almost as if I majored in Tristan Steele. Accepting my own sexuality was a difficult task to achieve; and now, I have another difficult one ahead. Seeing how I've come out and such, I'm tasked with reintroducing myself to family and friends. Thankfully I have God and Kendrick in my corner supporting me, because something tells me I'm going to need all the support I can get.

To Be Continued…

Going Forward

Want to find out what happens next for Tristan? Are you curious to know how his loved ones respond to his truth? Make sure you keep an eye out for the second installment of the *Majoring in Me* series, *Proclamation*.

And stop by www.accordingtot.com for book updates and other great content.

Ask For Help

If you or anyone you know is battling thoughts of suicide, or struggling with sexuality, please seek help. Below are several organizations offering a variety of resources and support to assist those suffering in the LGBT community. Save a life! Talk about it!

National Suicide Prevention Lifeline
Website: http://www.suicidepreventionlifeline.org/
Phone (For Immediate Assistance): 1-800-273-8255

GLBT National Help Center
Website: http://www.glbthotline.org/
GLBT National Youth Talkline Phone: 1-800-246-7743
GLBT National Hotline Phone: 1-888-843-4564
Email: help@GLBThotline.org

The Trevor Project
Website: http://www.thetrevorproject.org/
Trevor Line Phone (For Immediate Help): 1-866-488-7386
West Hollywood Office Phone: 310-271-8845
New York Office Phone: 212-695-8650
Email: info@thetrevorproject.org

Let's Talk LGBT (Presented by the National Black Justice Coalition)
Website: http://letstalklgbt.org/
Phone: 202-319-1552
Email: info@nbjc.org

It Gets Better Project
Website: http://www.itgetsbetter.org/
Email: info@itgetsbetter.org

Depressed Black Gay Men
Website: http://dbgm.org/
Email: info@dbgm.org

Made in the USA
Columbia, SC
18 December 2021